ABOUT THE AUTHOR

George G. Gilman was born in 1936 in what was then a small village east of London. He attended local schools until the age of fifteen. Upon leaving school he abandoned all earlier ambitions and decided to become a professional writer, with strong leanings towards the mystery novel. Wrote short stories and books during evenings, lunch hours, at weekends, and on the time of various employers while he worked for an international newsagency, a film company, a weekly book-trade magazine and the Royal Air Force.

His first short (love) story was published when he was sixteen and the first (mystery) novel ten years later. He has been a full-time writer since 1970, writing mostly Westerns which have been translated into a dozen languages and have sold in excess of 16 million copies. He is married and lives on the Dorset coast, which is as far west as he intends to move right now.

The STEELE series by George G. Gilman and published by New English Library:

ADAM STEELE 1: THE VIOLENT PEACE
ADAM STEELE 2: BOUNTY HUNTER
ADAM STEELE 3: HELL'S JUNCTION
ADAM STEELE 4: VALLEY OF BLOOD
ADAM STEELE 5: GUN RUN
ADAM STEELE 6: THE KILLING ART
ADAM STEELE 7: CROSS-FIRE
ADAM STEELE 8: COMMANCHE CARNAGE
ADAM STEELE 9: BADGE IN THE DUST
ADAM STEELE 10: THE LOSERS
ADAM STEELE 11: LYNCH TOWN
ADAM STEELE 12: DEATH TRAIL
ADAM STEELE 13: BLOODY BORDER
ADAM STEELE 14: DELTA DUEL
ADAM STEELE 15: RIVER OR DEATH
ADAM STEELE 16: NIGHTMARE AT NOON
ADAM STEELE 17: SATAN'S DAUGHTER
ADAM STEELE 18: THE HARD WAY
ADAM STEELE 19: THE TARNISHED STAR
ADAM STEELE 20: WANTED FOR MURDER
ADAM STEELE 21: WAGONS EAST
ADAM STEELE 22: THE BIG GAME
ADAM STEELE 23: FORT DESPAIR
ADAM STEELE 24: MANHUNT
ADAM STEELE 25: STEELE'S WAR: THE WOMAN
ADAM STEELE 26: STEELE'S WAR: THE PREACHER
ADAM STEELE 27: STEELE'S WAR: THE STOREKEEPER
ADAM STEELE 28: STEELE'S WAR: THE STRANGER
ADAM STEELE 29: THE BIG PRIZE
ADAM STEELE 30: THE KILLER MOUNTAINS
ADAM STEELE 31: THE CHEATERS
ADAM STEELE 32: THE WRONG MAN
ADAM STEELE 33: THE VALLEY OF THE SHADOW
ADAM STEELE 34: THE RUNAWAY
ADAM STEELE 35: STRANGER IN A STRANGE TOWN
ADAM STEELE 36: THE HELLRAISERS
ADAM STEELE 37: CANYON OF DEATH
ADAM STEELE 38: HIGH STAKES
ADAM STEELE 39: ROUGH JUSTICE
ADAM STEELE 40: THE SUNSET RIDE
ADAM STEELE 41: THE KILLING STRAIN
ADAM STEELE 42: THE BIG GUNFIGHT

The Hunted

George G. Gilman

NEW ENGLISH LIBRARY
Hodder and Stoughton

for
David Rider
who pointed out a problem
on which I had to get to grips!

A New English Library Original Publication, 1987

First New English Library Paperback Edition 1987

British Library C.I.P.

Gilman, George G.
The hunted.—(Adam Steele; 43)
Rn. Terry Harknett I. Title II. Series
823'.914[F] PR6058.A686/

ISBN 0-450-40846-9

The characters and situations in this book are entirely imaginary and bear no relation to any real person or actual happening

Printed and bound in Great Britain for Hodder and Stoughton Paperbacks, a division of Hodder and Stoughton Ltd., Mill Road, Dunton Green, Sevenoaks, Kent (Editorial Office: 47 Bedford Square, London, WC1 3DP) by Cox & Wyman Ltd., Reading, Berks.

1

It was the last Friday of the month, so the stage of the San Francisco and Central California company was scheduled to stop over at Providence. Because of this, an almost palpable air of anticipation permeated through the town in the timbered river valley which cut a north to south course through the western foothills of the Sierra Nevadas.

Providence was that kind of town: A community in which little of great consequence to anybody ever happened, outside of an infrequent birth, marriage or death. So many of the citizens of Providence looked forward eagerly to this day each month, irrespective of whether they had good reason to expect a mail delivery or knew somebody due to ride in on the stage. It broke the routine.

Even before people began to converge on a corner of the square at the north side of the scattered community there was a sense of gradually mounting excitement in the warming air of the summer morning. Long in advance of the scheduled arrival time of the stage, which was eleven o'clock. But it could get as late as one in the afternoon before anyone began to have serious doubts the Concord was not going to roll in off the north trail.

Today, as inevitably happened, those with time on their hands, or able to take time off from the daily chores, began to drift toward the north east corner of the large, sunlit square up to an hour before eleven. Some to gather into a garrulous group out front of the stage depot, others to kill the waiting time in the Golden Gate saloon: the two buildings with a gap between which formed the angle of the corner.

'Morning Harry, Harlan,' greeted the close to sixty years old, stockily built, near bald headed Roland Decker cheerfully, as he pushed between the creaking batwing doors of the saloon at the end of his ambling trek across from his meat market on the west side of the square. 'She going to be on time today, you think?'

He drew a curt nod of acknowledgement from Harlan Grout, the town's liveryman. Grout was not yet thirty, but always looked at least ten years older in the mornings: until he had tossed down enough straight shots of whiskey to cure his daily hangover. A once powerfully built man, he was now running to fat, had a drinker's ruddy complexion and hooded brown eyes with bloodshot surrounds flanking a sharply hooked nose.

'Maybe, maybe not,' Harry Krim replied to Decker. His tone was even and his expression amiable, competently concealing his wish to glower at the town butcher and snarl: How the frig would I know?

Krim, a red haired forty year old with broad shoulders and a pot belly, owned the Golden Gate and needed all the business he could get from a town in which drinkers were heavily outnumbered by citizens who did not enjoy liquor. So, almost invariably, he was polite to all his customers whether he liked them or not. Especially so on the morning of the last Friday of each month, when his business had a fillip, his takings rising in direct relation to the lateness of the stage.

He drew Decker a beer which was all the butcher ever drank at this time of day. And as he took the money for it he leaned across the bar counter to peer out of the window beside the batwings, his attention captured by the raised voices of two men. Then he scowled when he saw that Michael Morrison, who ran the stage depot with his mother, had greeted Ethan Brady as he stepped on to the threshold of his bank next door. Ethan hardly ever took a drink before the end of the working day and Morrison never took a drink at any time.

'Fine mornin', Mr Brady.'

'Sure is, Michael. How's your mother?'

'She's fine, Mr Brady.'

In the saloon, Decker muttered: 'I don't know why Ethan don't get himself hitched to Joanne Morrison. Seems to me, if they haven't actually been sparking since he became a widower, it's been the next thing to it.'

'There's a lot who'd agree with you, Roland,' Krim said as he heard footfalls outside. Then scowled when he saw the new arrivals were a trio of women, coming across from the stores on the west side of the square to form the start of a gossip circle out front of the stage depot.

'I reckon Mike would have somethin' to say about his Ma gettin' married again,' Harlan Grout said, obviously starting to feel better.

The short and ineffectual looking Morrison was, at thirty-five, a confirmed bachelor who doted on his skinny, unattractive and kindly mother.

'No doubting that, Harlan,' the butcher said, and took his drink with him to the window to peer out across the square, which was getting busier. As people with no other more pressing business than to wait for the stage emerged off Main Street where it came out of the thick timber forming the south side of the square.

'Ain't no doubtin', either, a big weddin' with all the trimmin's wouldn't do my business no harm,' Krim said grimly.

'Can't see Ethan springin' for that kinda shindig, Harry,' Grout answered as he set down his shot glass. After a moment's indecision he signalled for another drink to be poured, then he grinned and added: 'Now maybe if Adam Steele took the hints Susannah Lineker keeps droppin' right in front of his eyes, well then . . .' He shrugged.

'Hey now, Harlan,' Decker countered, and his expression of perturbation was not entirely mocking as he glanced over his shoulder toward the two men, one each side of the bar counter which ran along the right side wall of the small saloon with its sparse scattering of tables ringed by chairs. 'I wouldn't wish that female on my worst enemy.'

Krim countered: 'Come on, Decker. Steele ain't that to anyone in this town, and you know it.'

'Except Len, maybe?' Grout suggested.

Krim was about to take issue with this point, but Decker spoke first, after a double take through the window.

'Hey, there's Ellie Lineker just come out of the feed and seed store.' He vented a short, harsh laugh. 'If it's true what they say about a man needing to look at a woman's mother before he marries her, it explains why Susannah never has been able to stir up too much interest in men. Until she set her cap at the stranger.'

'Steele ain't hardly a stranger no more,' Krim argued.

'I'm with you, Harry,' Grout sided.

'Must be more than a year since he staked claim to the old Sanderson place?'

'Nearer to eighteen months,' Decker corrected and his tone of voice left no doubt he considered this was eighteen months too long.

Out front of the stage line depot, as the large clock above the caged counter in a corner of the waiting room chimed a quarter of eleven, a group composed entirely of women also abandoned earlier subjects of conversation. Lowered their voices to speak of the way in which the daughter of Jake and Ellie Lineker had, over the past couple of months, brazenly thrown herself at the man who had given a new lease of ranching life to the once derelict place out along Timber Creek.

This switch of subject, occasioned by the emergence of the farmer's wife from Mitchell Cody's store at the south west corner of the square, was abandoned before the less than handsome, painfully thin woman moved within earshot. Just before Rose Steiner from Mission Farm voiced the sardonic opinion that maybe Adam Steele was not away in Arizona at a horse sale so much as away from the Providence River Valley as the only means to escape the overpowering attentions of Susannah Lineker.

Then all whisperings ceased and tones altered from cynical to amicable as greetings and questions about her family were voiced to the plain-faced, work-wearied farmer's wife. Who, like most in the group, was only in the company of so many other women during the weekly church service—when there was little time afterwards for exchanges of news—and the last Friday of each month: when the atmosphere was more conducive to the kind of gossip the Reverend Joseph Marlow was likely to frown upon.

Within the next fifteen minutes, the cluster of women out front of the stage depot swelled, and was complemented by a few men. And Harry Krim tripled the number of his customers as other businessmen from the premises on three sides of the square hurried to the saloon. Having gotten away from their wives, or salved their own consciences with excuses of checking if there was anything for them on the stage.

There was Huey Attrill, who ran the *Providence Post-Despatch* from the building next to the saloon. Harold Archer, whose grocery store formed the angle of the square's north west corner with the school yard. Tom Knight, hen-pecked husband of Blanche who was the driving force of the boarding house next to Grout's Livery. Last to arrive was Len Fallows, the town sheriff who had an office across the alley from the newspaper building.

And thus, for a while, the Providence citizens who showed overt interest in the arrival of this month's stage were divided into two groups by more than just distance. Those out front of the depot were eager for the Concord to trundle in off the north trail between the law office and the meeting hall. And those in the saloon welcomed a delay for as long as it took them to drink their fill.

It was ten minutes after eleven by the clock in the depot when the four-horse team hauled the battered, travel-stained stagecoach on to the square at a less than headlong pace. By which time all but one of the men in the Golden Gate were pleased to see it as they crowded out between the batwings. Harry Krim, standing on the threshold of his place, chose to reserve his opinion: until after he knew if there were drinking-type passengers aboard.

There were certainly passengers, he glimpsed, as the slow-moving stage swung off the trail, headed toward his saloon and made a sharp turn to a stop out front of the depot. Passengers who, it was a safe bet, would get off in Providence. For this was as far south as the SF&CC line ran its stages. Here they turned around and headed north again, back up the trail to Broadwater, ten miles away. After that, to a host of small towns between here and San Francisco. It was seldom a long stop in Providence. The team was not changed here. And the drivers and shotguns never spent more time than they could help before they off-loaded what they had delivered and took aboard whatever Providence folks were sending north: always anxious to leave for Broadwater where they spent a night's holdover.

Krim, uncaring about the plans of the stage company men, had done a double-take through the windows of the Concord as it rolled past the doorway of the saloon. But there was no chance to confirm what he thought he had seen at first glance. It sure had looked to him, though, like a derby-hatted, grey-bearded man of forty or so threw a punch at the passenger seated opposite him. This was a woman of matching height and age who was fanning herself with a broad-brimmed, frilled hat as the blow landed.

Then the saloonkeeper saw only the back of the Concord as it completed its final turn. But he could see, also, the reactions of the people waiting at the depot as they did double-takes of their own at the pair inside the stage: expressed wide-eyed surprise or grinning amusement at what they witnessed. Maybe the throwing of another punch? For, a moment later, a shriek blasted out through the door window of the coach, open to catch the illusion of coolness in the slipstream during the ride through the late morning heat. The cry plenty loud enough to penetrate the background sounds of clopping hooves, creaking springs and clattering wheelrims just before the smiling driver hauled on the reins to bring the rig to a halt.

For several seconds there would have been silence on the square were it not for the birdsongs which filtered out of the trees to the south and the unsuccessful attempts of the shotgun rider to stifle his guffaws. Then:

'Why... you rotten, lousy, apology for a man, Elmer Rice!' the injured woman shrieked. 'Just who the hell do you think you are to hit me!'

The nearside door was flung open and the section of the waiting group which had been closing in on the stage suddenly back-tracked. Krim expected to see the furious woman lunge out, but it was the man who showed. Looking to be in a panic as he wrenched his head from side to side, like he was pleading for desperately needed help from the fervently watching crowd.

For a stretched second he remained like that, half-in half-out of the doorway, one arm stretched rigidly behind him. Then he gave vent to a shrill groan of pain, jerked his arm forward and leapt down. Would have pitched full length on the dusty, hard-packed ground had Ellie Lineker, Ethan Brady and Sheriff Fallows among others backed off faster. For the man banged into them, which halted his forward momentum and he was able to stay on his feet. Albeit swaying for several moments after he swung around to face the stage. Raised his right hand to suck at the blood which oozed out of a wound on the back of his bony wrist.

'How d'you like that as a taste of your own medicine, you bastard?' the woman roared from within the stage.

It drew gasps of righteous indignation from several of the women in the group, which were curtailed when Rice yelled back:

'Real strong medicine's what I'm in need of, seems to me!'

The woman appeared on the step of the Concord and chose to ignore him. Cast a contemptuous gaze over the array of faces ranged before her, apparently enjoying the way she had shocked the ladies of the town.

Rice snapped his head from side to side again, to ask: 'Place in town I can get me somethin' in case I caught the rabies off her?'

'It don't look like anyone can get much of any damn thing in this hick town, you bastard,' the woman sneered.

'Ma'am, I'd ask you to moderate your lan——' Len Fallows began to advise in a sternly placating tone. Turned fully toward her so she was certain to see the silver star pinned to his shirt pocket.

'Yeah, sheriff, you muzzle her!' Rice cut in eagerly. 'But you better be careful. Ever since before I married her I knew she was some kind of bitch. But I never known her to bite anyone before.'

2

Len Fallows, a year or two past fifty, was a tall, lean man with a sun-burnished face. His rough-hewn features were dominated by dark eyes and decorated by a black moustache.

He was as neatly dressed as usual and had a Frontier Colt in a holster tied down to his right thigh, the openly carried weapon as much a sign of his office as the badge pinned to his shirt front. He was the only local man on the square to carry a gun this way, and was probably the only Providence citizen there who was armed. And it seemed like he flaunted the fact as he swung away from the woman, faced the man: thrust his right hip forward, then withdrew it as he warned:

'The same goes for you, stranger! This is a decent town peopled by right-thinking folks. Our women don't like to hear foul language from anyone. Male or female.'

'My apologies, sheriff,' Elmer Rice offered. Tried a smile after he had grimaced at the sucked-dry bite on his wrist and glowered toward his wife who stepped down from the stage.

Krim saw confirmed they were of matching heights and about the same age. But here similarity ended. The man was slightly built and his five and a half feet frame probably weighed less than a hundred and forty pounds. He had the pale complexion of a man who spent far more time indoors than out. This pallor emphasised the dark, puffy half circles beneath his red-rimmed, bright blue eyes that perhaps suggested he was in permanent need of more sleep than he was allowed to have.

The neatly trimmed beard, an extension of his sideburns which were also grey, gave some kind of character to a face that otherwise would have been weak looking. He was dressed in a grey suit, white shirt, red necktie and black, high-buttoned boots which, with the derby, made him look like a citified dandy in his present surroundings. But the entire outfit had seen better days, a long time ago.

His red haired wife had fifty or more pounds on him, unevenly distributed at her bosom, hips and rear. Her face was maybe as pale as his, under the heavy layers of rouge and powder she had applied much earlier—before the morning stage ride had squeezed sweat from her pores. It was a face that expressed bitterness with the world in general, even in repose: the eyes narrowed by more than bright sunlight, the mouth line set in a soured twist that probably did not alter too much when she was in a better frame of mind.

Her neck-to-ankle, long-sleeved dress of pale blue was plainer than her hat and perhaps fitted her so snugly because she had put on weight since she purchased it. Certainly it had seen as much wear as her husband's outfit.

Elmer Rice went on: 'We've had a long and wearisome trip. I'm certain Lydia will be just as sorry as me that we've made such a bad first impression on the people of Providence when she's calmed down and——'

'I can do my own damn talkin'!' the woman broke in angrily. 'And I never say I'm sorry for bein' the way I am!'

Now she swung her head from side to side, treating the watchers to another glowering scrutiny that this time entailed a challenge to them to take issue with her. There was a tense pause of several seconds, filled by the shuffling of feet and the mumbling of reactions not loud enough to carry to the ears of the newcomers.

Then Michael Morrison asked: 'You got anythin' for us this time around, boys?'

'Guess you mean apart from the load of trouble we brought?' the young driver replied. Thudded a sharp elbow into the ribs of the twice as old shotgun who did not attempt to hold in a fresh gust of laughter.

Then they both climbed down from the high seat of the

Concord, the guard bringing with him a loosely packed carpetbag that was the only roof luggage. He handed this to Rice and spread a reflective frown across his face as he said:

'I got to tell you, mister. That was the most fun stretch of the whole trip between Frisco and here. Don't reckon me and my good buddy ever before heard a woman call her old man so many names for so long without hardly ever repeatin' herself.'

His mock earnestness was shattered by more laughter.

'Get about your business!' Lydia Rice snarled at him. 'And let's us get about ours, Elmer! Make the enquiries! Need me a drink. That's if this here straitlaced town allows a woman into the saloon?'

Harry Krim spread across his face a smile that looked mostly of pleasure, just a little of avariciousness. He stepped outside the Golden Gate, held open one of the batwings and executed an elaborate bow, accompanied by a sweep of his arm as he offered: 'Step right this way, lady. Ain't no-one I'd rather have in my place more than a high-spirited woman who knows her own mind.'

Krim figured that Lydia Rice in the saloon was just the bait. For he guessed a whole bunch of local citizens were sure to follow, eager to learn more about her and her husband after their fighting arrival in Providence.

And so it proved, for no sooner had the statuesque redhead swept over the threshold than the group at the stage became separated into two again. One section bustled into the Golden Gate while the larger proportion remained at the depot. Some doubtless hopeful that the mailsack and packages which the guard, the driver and Morrison took from the Concord's boot contained items for them. Others simply wanting to hear from the stage men news of events outside the close confines of Providence.

The liveryman had intended to go and join those who hurried into the saloon. But he was halted in his tracks when, after listening to something Elmer Rice said to him, the sheriff called:

'Hey, Harlan. Rice here wants to rent a couple of horses. See he gets what he wants, uh? Show these strangers this town's not such a hick, no-account place as they seem to think it is.'

'Lydia thinks, sir!' the diminutive man hurried to correct. Smiled broadly as he peered around the square, breathing deeply of the timber-scented air. 'Looks to be a fine place to me.' Now he studied the people who were close to him, nodding his approval. 'Filled with real nice folks, I'll be bound. Just the kinda place where me and the missus will be happy to settle.'

'Settle?' Rose Steiner echoed, an expression of disbelief emphasising her myriad wrinkles.

Those who were about to go into the stage depot, trailing the three men toting the mail and freight, came to an abrupt halt and stared back, intrigued. As Harlan Grout, who had become more eager to do some horse renting business than to begin laying the groundwork for tomorrow's hangover, paused as he was about to beckon for Rice to follow him toward the livery. There was even a sudden end to much talk in the Golden Gate: so it was possible to hear from outside when Lydia Rice growled her requirements to Harry Krim.

'Draught of beer and a shot on the side, barkeep. No, leave the damn bottle!'

Elmer Rice replied to Mrs Steiner, his grin broadening as he moved after Grout: 'Sure thing, ma'am. Settle close to town, anyway. Understand the Trail's End Ranch is a little ways out to the north. That right?'

'Trail's End?' Fallows repeated tautly. 'The old Sanderson place?'

Rice thrust an upturned thumb in the air. 'Got it in one, Sheriff. Lydia's name's Rice since she got hitched to me, naturally. But before, it was Sanderson. She's the sole survivin' kin of the family that owned the place way back. We've come here to claim her inheritance.'

'But somebody's already livin' out there,' Ellie Lineker countered with a puzzled frown, shaking her head.

People in the saloon crowded to the doorway and

window, abruptly far more interested in Elmer Rice than his wife. Until the redhead recaptured attention. Snarled:

'Yeah, so we heard up in Broadwater! Some cheatin' claim jumper who just moved on in with no by-your-leave to anyone!'

'Steele by name, we heard,' her husband added with a sneer. 'And steal by nature, it seems.'

'He ain't out at the place right now,' Ethan Brady said warily. The banker was a short and flabby man, near to sixty years old and prone to imagined nervous sweating for the least reason. He mopped now at his brow and rubbed at his neck with an already damp handkerchief.

'Best he don't try to come back!' Lydia Rice warned menacingly.

'On account of if he does,' her husband augmented with a hardening of his eyes as he hefted the carpetbag in a meaningful gesture, 'he'll wish he'd stayed away!'

Brady mopped more vigorously and some of those who saw this probably guessed the banker had loaned Steele the money to finance his horse trading trip.

This as Rice spread the grin back across his face, signalled to Grout he was ready to go see the horses that were available for rent from the town livery.

In the Golden Gate, his wife took the first whiskey at a purposeful swallow, began to sip at the beer as she poured a second.

And the crowd which had gathered to witness the more eventful than usual arrival of the stage began to break up still more.

'Goddamn Steele!' Len Fallows muttered with a scowl cutting deep lines into his bronzed face as he directed an embittered gaze skywards.

The craggy-faced Widow Kenway, who owned the hardware store and also acted as the town barber, said sadly: 'It seems to me, Len, the way that man has had so much trouble brought to his door the Almighty can't damn him no more than He already has.'

The lawman, most unlike him, seemed to be about to spit.

Then he emerged from a private world of soured introspection: sheepishly realised he was still surrounded by friends and neighbours of long standing. He swallowed the saliva, but was not prepared to let this take the full heat out of his ill feelings for the Virginian.

'Beg pardon, Faith,' he growled. 'But given the choice between Steele and anyone else, I'll take anyone else.'

The recently widowed Faith Kenway, who was probably the ugliest woman in Providence, had a reputation for second sight. But as she eyed the lawman morosely and shook her head slowly, she was simply expressing an opinion when she told him: 'Reckon there ain't so many hereabouts are as ready to agree with you on that as there used to be, Len.'

'That's right, Len,' Ethan Brady agreed, low enough for just the Widow Kenway and the sheriff to hear him. 'And they're bitter words if you find you have to eat them.'

'Maybe,' Fallows allowed grimly. Then cracked his mouth and eyes in a cruel grin as he added: 'But if Steele gets his just deserts, it'll taste mighty sweet to me.'

3

Lydia Rice tossed back three shots of rye while she was drinking the beer and successfully parrying the more probing questions put to her by the owner and the other customers in the Golden Gate Saloon. Those questions, anyway, she considered had answers which were no business of the inquisitors.

She managed this without actually telling Harry Krim, Roland Decker, Harold Archer, Huey Attrill and a trio of out of town farmers in so many words to mind their own business. For the most part she deftly sidestepped the queries she had no intention to answer straight. Supplied sometimes sardonically humorous responses to those that, to her mind, were not private.

Thus did she create a good impression on the men who learned so little of any consequence from her.

She was related only distantly to the Sandersons. The old man had been an uncle of her mother: or something like that. But she and Elmer had done some deep digging and there were no other living relatives: closer or even more distant.

There was nothing so out of the ordinary about the fight between herself and Elmer. They were always fighting, and as often as not he threw punches at her. Usually she was fast enough to duck out of the way. Like the one he had thrown as the stage rolled on to the square. Look at her face, there was no sign of a bruise.

He did land a kick on her shin, though. And she undecorously raised the hem of her dress to reveal the discoloured swelling on the front of her fleshy left leg.

But she sure as hell had paid him back with interest when

she sank her teeth into his skinny wrist.

The row had got started because he was for selling up her inheritance in whatever state it happened to be, while she wanted to see if they could make a go of it. But Elmer was city born and bred. And she came from the mid-West corn belt.

So, Lydia Rice could have ridden out of Providence after doing much to repair the first bad impression she and her husband made when they arrived in town. By the time she was halfway through the third rye, her tongue was loosening as her thinking got increasingly fluid. The mood in the saloon was lightening to her lead and there was an increasing amount of easy laughter: loud and genuine, which caused some shock among the dispersing crowd outside.

But then Huey Attrill made it known to Lydia Rice he was the editor and publisher of the *Providence Post-Despatch*. Requested: 'I surely would like the privilege of a private interview with you, ma'am. So I could run a piece in the paper about——'

'A friggin' reporter?' the redhead snarled as she whirled on the slightly built, middle-aged man.

The intense expression suddenly slid off Attrill's angular features and he backed hurriedly away from the woman: looked as scared as had Elmer Rice while he struggled to tear free of her grip and get clear of the stage. It was almost as if the newspaperman was driven backwards by some palpable force generated by the glare of the incensed woman.

'Editor and publisher, ma'am,' Attrill blurted defensively.

'You sneaky bastard!' she snarled. Finished her drink and for a moment held the glass like she intended to hurl it into Attrill's terrified face. He backed off from her some more. 'I loathe and detest newspapermen! My first husband was one of them. You can't say nothin' to a newspaperman without he twists it and . . . Get out of my friggin' way!'

Because he was in a direct line between her and the batwings, Huey Attrill had to step aside: for it was obvious she was not going to deviate from her chosen path.

Once past him, she began to yell her husband's name, bellowing it at the top of her voice. And it happened that Elmer Rice was just emerging from the livery, leading two ready-saddled geldings, as his wife slammed out between the batwings.

By then the men in the saloon formed the largest gathering: the majority of those who had remained outside long gone about their business. Some carrying mail or goods brought by the stage, most with just a mixture of facts, fictions and opinions based upon what they had seen and heard.

For a few moments, those still moving on the square slowed to the sound of the raised voice. But there was nothing more of interest to be gleaned. The Rices met up alongside the stage, exchanged terse words that were not loud enough to carry more than a few feet, then got astride the horses. Rode across the square and on to the north trail where it commenced between the meeting hall and the law office. The grey-bearded and tired-eyed man who looked suddenly close to exhaustion, gazed directly ahead: seemingly deep in thought. But the redhead cast a final glance over the square before she rode off it: her expression directing tacit contempt at all who chose to meet her glittering, unblinking gaze.

For a few minutes after clopping hooves had faded down the timber-flanked trail there was an insistent buzz of many conversations as the events of the morning were recounted, people questioning each other and trading opinions about the Rices and how Adam Steele was likely to react to their claim to ownership of the Trail's End spread.

It soon emerged, to much disgruntlement, that the men in the saloon had learned little of any additional interest from the woman: and Harlan Grout had not even attempted to draw anything out of Elmer Rice. He'd been too eager to raise cash on the rent of the horses to finance more drinking sessions in the Golden Gate, was the peevish consensus. The guard off the stage gave it as his opinion that maybe there was a heavy weapon of some kind—a shotgun most likely—in the carpetbag. In all other respects the Rices, who had boarded at Broadwater, travelled extremely light.

Then it was midday, and Miss Lavinia Attwood released her abruptly boisterously noisy students from the one class-room schoolhouse. The driver turned the Concord around and drove out of town in the wake of the Rices, he and the guard relishing a night off in the much more lively town ten miles to the north. Harry Krim had just Harlan Grout to serve, for the rest of his customers had left the saloon to return to their business premises and farms.

The intriguing new arrivals were not so much forgotten as pushed to the backs of people's minds as the routine of day to day living in a small town was resumed. The couple who maintained they had legal claim to the old Sanderson place were discussed from time to time. But with no more emphasis than news of Broadwater and other towns north to San Francisco or state and national topics that the driver and guard had made mention of during their brief stopover. Along with items of general interest contained in the small bundle of personal letters from far off relatives and friends which had arrived in the mailsack.

Which Miss Attwood, taking lunch at the boarding house where she had a room, found infuriating. She was a tall and thin woman of something over fifty with sharp features and severely styled grey hair. A prim and proper spinster, she seldom got ruffled, unless in the schoolhouse when the children were particularly fractious. But Blanche Knight, the short and obese woman who was her friend as well as her landlady, came extremely close to feeling the sharp edge of the schoolma'am's tongue during lunch in the dining room of the boarding house. This when Mrs Knight had repeated several times, with a mounting irritation of her own, that she knew nothing of the newly arrived couple except that the foul-mouthed Lydia Rice apparently had legal claim to Trail's End.

Later, as Miss Attwood was re-crossing the brightly sunlit

square toward the schoolhouse to commence afternoon lessons, her carriage even more rigidly erect than usual because of the depth of her feelings, she hurried to intercept Len Fallows. And the sheriff, heading back to his office after going home for lunch, caused her even more exasperation when he admitted he had not asked to see proof of what the Rices claimed. Nor was Miss Attwood's humour improved when Fallows irritably reminded her of an indisputable fact: when Adam Steele moved in on the Trail's End spread, no-one had asked him what right he had to do so.

It was already more than a minute past one o'clock, but the normally punctual Miss Attwood caused herself further delay while the children raucously enjoyed extra recess time in the schoolyard. She detoured to the front of the hardware store where Faith Kenway was opening up after the break. Said bitterly:

'It would suit Len Fallows down to the ground if Adam were to lose the place! No matter what the circumstances!'

'Quite so, Lavinia,' the Widow Kenway agreed, preoccupied. Then spoke of what was worrying her. 'What about Arlene and Billy?'

Miss Attwood shook her head to the query which referred to the black woman who cooked and cleaned house part time for Steele and the mentally retarded man who worked out at the place every day but spent the nights with the Reverend Joseph Marlow and his wife. 'It's not one of Arlene's days to be there. And while Adam's away Billy only goes out mornings and evenings to attend to the stock.'

'So there shouldn't be any trouble until . . ?' The ugly widow woman allowed her voice to trail away as she chewed on her lower lip.

'I'll ensure Arlene and Billy are warned to stay away, Faith,' Miss Attwood said firmly. Added, a little anxiously: 'Adam was not sure precisely what his plans would be. But it cannot be too long now before he returns.'

She turned to go toward the open wrought-iron gates in the stone front wall of the schoolyard. And as soon as she had called the children to order and shepherded them into the schoolhouse, the usual afternoon tranquillity settled on the square that was the down-town area of Providence.

In the heat of the day birdsongs from the trees to the south and the small sounds of commercial business from the buildings on the other three sides kept the silence from being absolute. Infrequently, muffled noises of men working on places far off in the timber reached the square. But nothing untoward. Certainly the clop of hooves as a horse was ridden slowly along Main Street from the south was no cause for concern: until those who happened to glance toward the rider saw he was another stranger and some of them experienced moments of anxiety.

Lavinia Attwood was among the first to see the rider, when she went to one of the classroom windows to look out across the yard and the square. Having heard the horse while she was moving among the desks, patrolling to ensure the older students did not crib from others as they worked on an arithmetic test while the younger ones concentrated on drawing a farmyard scene with coloured crayons.

At first she hoped it would be Adam Steele, then changed her mind. For the sooner he got back, the sooner matters would come to a certainly unfortunate and possibly violent head at Trail's End. But even before she removed the spectacles she needed for close work and was thus able to see the rider in sharp focus, she knew he was not Steele. For the Virginian had been determined to bring back a stallion and some mares with which to commence breeding out at the ranch.

She had been thinking a great deal about Adam Steele during the start of the afternoon lessons. About the man who, it had to be admitted, had squatted out on the old Sanderson place. Now, as she turned from the window and reset the spectacles on the bridge of her nose, went to sit at her desk at the front of the quiet classroom, she could not keep herself from thinking about him again.

She was sure she knew why he had spent so much time,

effort and money on Trail's End before he left it to go buy the horses which were his reason for getting the place into such fine shape. And although he had not admitted it to her in so many words, neither had he denied that she was correct in her assumption.

Certainly she knew more about Adam Steele than most people hereabouts, for she had been one of his staunchest allies almost from the first moment he arrived as a stranger.

Since then he had devoted a year and a half to transforming the virtually derelict ranch into a fine piece of land on which a hard-working man could make a good living. The house, the barn and the corral were all fixed up now. And a fence enclosed the something over three and a half thousand acres of good growing and grazing land: high and strong enough to keep in the horses he intended to raise. Steele and Billy Baxter had dug a small lake so that even if Timber Creek ran dry in drought, the stock could be kept watered for several weeks. Two fields were planted with crops to make the Trail's End Ranch self-sufficient in vegetables. And there was a hog, a milk cow, a rooster and a dozen hens. Tools and machinery had been purchased to take the drudgery out of some of the work. Then, suddenly, all the place needed was a bunch of breeding stock.

Lavinia Attwood knew for a fact Steele had been a rootless drifter after the War Between the States ended the good life he had enjoyed as the son and heir of one of the richest plantation owners in Virginia. She could only make an educated guess about how harsh and violent his life had been as he moved from one ill-starred piece of country to another: until he came upon the appropriately named Trail's End. Which he decided to transform into the closest he was going to get to his ideal—a substitute for all that he had lost back in Virginia.

From an occasional remark he made, the schoolma'am knew there had been other times when Steele thought he had found his ideal. But always it had been taken from him or he had chosen to ride away from it for reasons he never specified. He spoke very little of his past, so it was only somebody with perception, allied to more than passing interest—such as Lavinia Attwood—who was able to make such an educated guess as to why the Virginian had taken so long to go buy his horses.

He was anxious, even afraid, that the run of good fortune and relative peace he was enjoying would be broken as soon as he took that final step toward the establishment of his ideal.

And so it could prove to be, if Elmer and Lydia Rice were able to provide proof of legal title to Trail's End.

But there was still a little time left for Steele to relish his new life style, for the moment blissfully ignorant of the trouble that was awaiting him at the place out along Timber Creek. As he rode toward Providence in the wake of this stranger.

One by one, other people's attention was drawn to look toward the rider. And all failed to identify him as he crossed the square, angling slightly from a direct north route to head toward the law office. A handsome young man astride a fine-looking horse: the both of them showing signs of long and wearying travel since the start of the day. And doubtless before then, for it was a lot of miles from anywhere to the south of Providence.

Seated behind his desk in the law office, Len Fallows was one of the last to interrupt what occupied him to look toward the stranger. He realised immediately it was not Steele and, just like Miss Attwood, he was in two minds about how to react to this fact. It would be good to get the matter of ownership of Trail's End out of the way as soon as possible. But the Rices were obviously troublemakers and Steele, while for most of the time he could be as law-abiding as the next man, was inclined to meet fire with fire in certain circumstances.

On balance, he thought he would prefer to get this Trail's End mess over and done with as fast as possible. So he found himself resenting the good looking young stranger simply because he was not Adam Steele. And his ill-humour increased when the newcomer reined in his piebald gelding out front of the law office and hunched low to peer in through the window, then swung down from his saddle.

Fallows was drafting a letter to the telegraph company, putting forward the town's case for an extension of the wire from Broadwater to Providence, and he had just thought of a stylish way to phrase a particularly telling point. But it was driven out of his mind when he saw that the stranger intended to enter his office. His expression was just short of a frown and the tone of his voice barely polite as he said to the man who followed in the opening door:

'Afternoon to you. Something I can do?'

He saw at once that the newcomer was not so handsome close to as he had seemed at a distance. Nor so young. He was past thirty, of medium build without an ounce of excess flesh on his hard-packed body and muscular limbs, nor his long, lantern-jawed face. It was the easy way he carried himself that created the impression of youth. The cold glint in his dark eyes and the slightly twisted set of his thin lips detracted from handsomeness.

His all black, Western style clothing was old and worn under a powdering of dust that was crusted where it adhered to sweat-sodden areas of the fabric. He carried a Frontier Colt in a holster tied down to his right thigh, in the same manner as did Fallows. But this man's revolver, holster and bullet-heavy gunbelt had seen longer, rougher use.

'I'm lookin' for the Trail's End Ranch, man,' the stranger said, his tone as hard as his looks. Removed his hat to reveal a fine crop of tightly curled red hair. Scattered dust on the floor that Arlene Forrester scrupulously cleaned three times a week. Ran his shirt sleeve across his sweat-sheened brow. Glanced around the neat office like something outside of himself smelled bad.

In the few moments it took for the travel-stained, tough-looking stranger to accomplish this and replace his hat, Len Fallows forgot thoughts of literary composition and the benefits to be gained from the telegraph coming through to Providence. As he tried not to let his imagination run away with him about the scale of potential trouble concerned with the old Sanderson place.

'Before I give you that information, I'd like to have you answer a question or two, Mr . . ?'

He put down the pen and flipped closed the well lid on the ink stand. Watched as the man who was a fresh factor in the looming mess over Trail's End vented a sigh, shrugged, half turned to swing the door closed and then approached the chair in front of the desk in his loose-limbed gait.

'Well, I'll tell you, man,' he replied, speaking in a lazy drawl as the hardness drained out of him: to reveal something of his bone-deep weariness as he made to lower himself gratefully into the chair.

But that was not his intention. His intention was to lull the wide awake, neatly attired, suspicious lawman into a false sense of security. Have him, after he was obviously perturbed at the mention of Trail's End, think he was in command of the situation which had been brought into his office.

'What the——' Fallows started to snarl. But suddenly was in no position to make demands.

For the stranger had lunged into a lightning-fast move. Sprung out of the state of weariness that was only part faked, to launch an arrogantly confident attack on the sheriff. He had not dropped more than an inch toward the chair before he straightened. Leaned forward across the desk. As his right hand reached to grasp a bunch of Fallows' shirt front, and the left seemed to lean on the desk top for support. But as he straightened up again and took a step back, the hand moved. Reached for and yanked from the holster the lawman's revolver. This as Fallows was dragged up out of his chair to be jerked, face down, across the desk: the crown of his head pressed against the hard, flat belly of his assailant.

He had started to snarl a curse. And to struggle: flailing his arms in a desperate effort to wrench himself free of the younger man's grip. But even before he realised his gun was gone from the holster, he felt the hard circle of a muzzle pressed into the sparsely fleshed side of his neck.

He froze and was dumbstruck as the man reiterated in the same easy-going, drawling voice as before:

'Well, I'll tell you, man. When I ask a question, I don't like to have another one tossed back at me.'

As Fallows craned his neck, to look up out of the corner of his eye at his captor he expected a painful counter move to keep him from doing so. But the man, hard-eyed and brutal-mouthed again, had no objection. The sheriff said hoarsely:

'Okay, you've shown what a tough customer you are. So what now?'

'Same question, man. How do I get to the Trail's End Ranch?'

'If I don't tell you, you'll kill me with my own handgun, right?'

After his initial shock at the sudden attack, Len Fallows felt strangely calm. He had never been gunshot. But not too long ago he had been savagely knifed and had nearly died. It had been touch and go. Neither at the time nor since had he ever considered it a useful experience: the awareness of being so dangerously close to death. Now, although he recognised the craziness of it, he was certain the time of hovering on the brink of death was standing him in good stead in this tense, perilous situation. For he was not so scared as he would have been had he not had that close brush with the ending of his life.

But he had to guard against making a reckless counter-move, he knew this.

'What?' the stranger came back, obviously troubled by the unexpectedly calm reaction of the country town sheriff he had at his mercy.

'I said——'

'I heard what you friggin' said, man!' He seemed stuck for what to say next, gained some time by thumbing back the hammer of the Colt.

Fallows' mind was working smoothly and his senses seemed oddly heightened. He had taken apart, cleaned and re-assembled the revolver often enough to be familiar with every component of it. And now he heard the individual clicks of each move in the sequence, as the cocking of the hammer activated the pawl and ratchet to rotate the cylinder and align the next loaded chamber with the firing pin.

'So?' he asked, and heard the more pronounced huskiness in his voice. Felt dampness on many areas of his body as sweat oozed from the pores. It had been a bad idea to meet the bullyboy tactics of the stranger with such calmness, and now he was not sure he could maintain a grip on his self-control for too long while he stayed trapped in the helpless and humiliating face down attitude across the desk.

The scar on his chest where the knife blade had sunk so deep was beginning to throb. Probably all in his mind, he guessed: rather than as a result of true physical pain. As the silence lengthened, his worry increased. He was getting as scared as the hoarseness of his voice and the dampness on his skin made him seem. He could be forced into making some stupidly reckless move before the confused stranger killed him out of hand.

'So just tell me what I want to know, man,' his captor said at length. His tone less hard now as he eased the pressure of the gun muzzle against Fallows' flesh. 'You got me mad. I get mad real easy when I'm this bushed. It's been a long, hard slog to get here. Last thing I wanted was trouble with a hick town lawman.

'If there'd been anyone else around, I'd have asked them. Somebody out on that crazy Main Street of yours that's like a friggin' trail, way it winds through the woods.

'But it's like bein' back in friggin' Mexico, man. Everyone takes a *siesta* in the afternoons, uh? I seen you in here. It's a little closer than the saloon. And in the saloon I'd be tempted to have a drink I don't have the time for.

'Like I don't have the time for this shit, man. Just tell me where Trail's End is. And I'll be on my way. I'm really bushed, you know?'

His voice got softer as he spoke the words with widening gaps between them. So he rambled, like a man close to falling into a exhausted sleep. At the same time, the pressure of the gun muzzle eased still more. And maybe the grip on the shirt front was loosened, too.

The sheriff still had his head screwed around so he could look up into the bristled, dust-smudged, sweat-sheened face of the stranger: which expressed a degree of fatigue totally in keeping with his voice and manner. Now he said, covertly tensing himself to follow his words with violent actions:

'You go out on the north trail which starts between this building and the meeting hall. You'll pass a few spurs to the left and right but don't take any until you've ridden a half mile. The river and the trail come close then, and a creek cuts in from the west. A side trail fords the river and heads off up the slope alongside Timber Creek. That's the spur that dead ends at the old Sanderson place. Trail's End.'

The stranger let go of Fallows' shirt front and withdrew the revolver. He looked even closer to exhaustion as the sheriff turned his head away: prepared to hurl himself up off the desk at the same time as he made a grab for his gun in the other man's hand. But again, just as when the stranger had seemed about to drop into the chair, he fooled the lawman.

Even before a single muscle in Fallows' tall lean frame—which was not so young as it used to be—began to respond to the commands of his brain, the stranger had swung fluidly into action again. Hooked a thumb over the top of the hammer to prevent an accidental firing as he raised and brought down the revolver: to crash the underside of the barrel and the triggerguard into the back of Fallows' head.

The Providence sheriff was aware of a split second of excruciating agony, like his skull had exploded. Then he was swallowed up by a pitch blackness that smothered all feeling. He lay limply, arms at his sides, legs draped behind the desk and his head hanging over the front. A little blood stained his black, grey-streaked hair. The breath was sucked in and vented out of his mouth with just a trace of laboured harshness.

The stranger dropped to his haunches and pressed the muzzle of the revolver into the centre of the bloodstained area: twisted the Colt one way, then the other. It was not a sadistic act. He was merely checking to see that Len Fallows did not react: was certainly unconscious, not just playing possum.

So the weary-eyed man, again slow-moving, was able to place the revolver on the desk beside its unfeeling owner. Knew there would be no problem about getting out of this jerk-water town before the alarm was raised.

He crossed to the door, swung it open and then paused to look back at the figure slumped over the desk. Spoke to Fallows, not especially acting the part of an innocent visitor taking his leave for any prying small-town eyes which might be watching. Said sardonically:

'Mostly I'm not called Mister anythin', man. Usually it's just plain Curly. Guess when you wake up hurtin' bad, though, you'll think of a few different kinds of name for me.'

4

Adam Steele was past forty, but sometimes he looked to be several years younger. When his face spread with a boyish grin. And the light was not too good. As it was when he neared the southern fringe of Providence, feeling in the right frame of mind for that kind of grin.

It was a face which had been nondescriptly handsome in the past, with a lean structure and regular features: the coal black eyes that might have conveyed hardness cancelled out by the gentle line of the mouth. But over the years since the War Between the States had robbed him of his birthright, harsh times that had far outnumbered the easy ones had gradually moulded his features into a more distinguished shape. A process helped by the premature greying of the once red hair that had commenced even before he left his father's plantation to fight for the Confederate Cause.

Not just his facial features had changed. Neither had the toughening up process of his experiences in the brutal war and during the much longer violent peace acted only to harden his less-than-powerful frame—he stood little more than five and a half feet tall and weighed a solid one hundred and sixty pounds. His character had altered radically, too: as he underwent the transformation from a privileged rich kid with all that that entailed into a man of violence. Ready to kill without remorse if his survival depended upon it.

And he had killed. Often. With the Colt Hartford revolver action rifle that was the sole inheritance from his father, the knife he carried concealed in a boot sheath, a kerchief that was actually an Oriental weapon of strangulation, and any other conventional or improvised weapon that came to hand.

All that was behind him now, though. Some of it not so far in the past, for violence had not been entirely banished from his life since he came to this town and chose to put down roots on a piece of abandoned land to the north.

But there would be no more of it. He felt confident of that. And his determination to ensure this expanded as he drew closer to the town in the timber, his boyish grin broadening when he looked over his shoulder at the string of three mares and a stallion that trailed his gelding on a lead line.

Fine breeding stock he had purchased at a fair price, after some haggling, from a trader west of Fort Yuma. All the horses in good health, all with the proper papers which registered their transfer by sale to Adam Steele, Trail's End, Providence, California.

Afternoon had totally retreated in the crimson wake of the setting sun and it was the time of evening on the brink of full moonlit night when Steele rode off the red dirt open trail and on to the southern end of Main Street. Started to feel especially good now, as he relished the sense of returning to familiar surroundings he had missed while he was gone from them.

There was no-one out of doors at this supper time of day as he rode past the stone-walled cemetery with the white-painted clapboard church in a rear corner. Then between the rows of one and two storey houses that stretched a short way beyond the graveyard before the street began a meandering course through the timber toward the square, a whole mile to the north.

The day's work was over now: except, perhaps, for Joe Marlow, who was maybe working in the parlour of the house next to the church on his sermon for next Sunday. Soon the preacher, like the people in the other seven houses that flanked this end of Main Street, would sit down to eat the food the Virginian could smell, the appetising cooking aroma permeating the acrid taint of woodsmoke which rose through the still air from a chimney of every house.

The church was the only building in total darkness.

Elsewhere, light glimmered at cracks where drapes failed to meet: while in two instances entire windows were squared with lamplight. One of these was darkened by the dousing of a lamp. At the other, a man appeared. Just a silhouette against the brightness. This at the Marley house, so the man would be Josh Marley who owned an out of town farm he rented to the Lineker family.

The Linekers, who were the only fly in Steele's ointment, he reflected briefly as the name flipped into his mind. Or rather, Susannah, the daughter of Jake and Ellie Lineker. She was getting to be an irritating nuisance and he knew that soon he would have to take some kind of drastic action to discourage her interest in him. Even though it went against his grain to be anything less than a gentleman toward women.

Then he put the problem of Susannah out of his mind. For he wanted nothing to mar how good he felt tonight. And he was about to tip his hat in greeting toward Josh Marley. But the man abruptly stretched a hand to either side. Jerked the curtains across the window with a gesture that, intended or not, strongly suggested he wanted to block his view of the night outside rather than to preserve his domestic privacy.

And Steele suddenly lost the sense of well being he had brought with him into Providence. For he now realised he was under surreptitious surveillance from other windows. Some of them in unlit rooms. Being watched with varying degrees of mistrust. Or, if not mistrust, something very similar. Allied with hostility, even.

Which was not a new experience for him, for he had met with such tacit ill-feeling many times in the past. But this was inevitably when he rode into strange towns. Where decent and law abiding citizens felt they had good reason to be wary of a lone saddletramp who regarded them with much the same degree of suspicion as they viewed him.

Hell, it *had* happened more than once here in Providence: after he first decided to put down roots at Trail's End and needed to visit town for supplies every now and then. And a couple of times had been involved in the worst kind of trouble. But the way he had handled himself during the violence, and how he had lived peaceably out on the spread in the periods between had acted to win over many of the local people who at the outset had been dead set against him for trying to settle in the Providence River Valley.

So what could have happened to alter the situation from how it had been when he left to go south on the horse-buying trip? What possible brand of trouble could have arisen that was evidently laid at his door during his absence?

He briefly contemplated halting his mount and the string of three mares and a stallion. To dismount and go ask somebody what was wrong. At the Marlow house would be best. There, if the preacher or his wife were reluctant to give him the information he sought, then Billy Baxter surely would do the best he could. Billy lived in a stable out back of the house, but he was allowed inside to eat supper with the Marlows.

But if Billy was in the house now, about to tuck in to another fine meal prepared by Jane Marlow, why had he not made his presence known? The man of more than thirty years with the mind of a child of six or seven would not usually be able to contain his excitement in such a circumstance: the return after many days of the Virginian he virtually hero worshipped.

So if Billy wasn't where he normally could be found at this time of day..? Maybe the trouble was caused by him? Or in some other way involved the mentally deficient man? And those who kept covert watch on Steele were not so much concerned to see him back as afraid to face him with news of what had happened while he was away?

Then he rode off this straight stretch of Main Street, and started around the first curve among the pines and live oaks, birches and maples, spruces and willows, that extended up to the town square. Here and there he crossed intersections with side lanes that led out to scattered small farms and ranches, some with occasional isolated houses set back from them among the timber.

The house of Len and Molly Fallows was on Fir Tree Road, close to the corner with Main. The sheriff, Steele knew, would never view him with anything other than resentment and suspicion. And would enjoy revealing the reason for the less than warm welcome home the town was giving Steele.

Tonight there was a light in an upstairs bedroom as well as the parlour, and the Virginian wondered if the lawman or his wife was sick. As far as he could tell, the sound of the hooves of the five slow-moving horses did not draw anyone to peer out of the Fallows house.

Out of sight at the end of a track off Mission Farm Road which cut away from Main to the west, was the crude shack where Arlene Forrester lived. Alone once more after Zachery Petrie, the baby son of her dead niece had been adopted and taken back east. If Steele chose to make the detour the black woman was sure to be home and she would certainly hold nothing back of what she knew of the cause of the tacit hostility directed at him.

But, without doubt, the most concise and clear explanation was likely to come from Lavinia Attwood, the schoolma'am who had taken a kind of maternal interest in the Virginian. And since she had a room at the Knight boarding house on the town square, to see her would not involve any time-consuming sidetracking into the timber.

As he expected when he rode clear of the trees, all but one of the buildings on the other three sides of the square were either in total darkness or showed just chinks of light at draped windows. The exception was the Golden Gate Saloon which announced it was open for business with lamplight which spilled out over and under the batwing doors and through the uncurtained window.

As usual at this supper time of the day there were no horses hitched to the rail out front of the saloon. Also not unusual, at any time of the day, Harlan Grout was in the saloon. He appeared on the threshold to peer across the moonlit square, seeking the cause of the thud of many hooves.

The liveryman paced his day-long drinking to hold a level of drunkenness that seldom seriously blurred his thinking. He immediately recognised Steele and half turned, obviously to relay news of his discovery. And before the Virginian had covered half the distance between the end of Main Street and the two storey house with a ROOMS FOR RENT sign fixed above the porch, Harry Krim had come out from behind his bar counter to join his only customer in the doorway.

'You've got a problem, Mr Steele!' the saloonkeeper called, his voice loud enough to be heard above the clatter of hooves that was the only obtrusive body of sound in the night. Krim's tone expressed genuine concern because of the bad news he was about to reveal.

Steele brought his horses to a halt before the boarding house and the door in the porch was opened so that another shaft of light sprawled out to compete with the glow of the moon. And the Virginian replied to Krim as he turned to look across the porch:

'I've been getting that message ever since I hit town, feller.'

As he eyed the two people on the threshold of the boarding house he sensed more watchers, from the line of stores on the opposite side of the square: the people who lived out back of their business premises drawn to the front by the shouted words. He explained to Lavinia Attwood, who frowned at him and the broadly grinning Billy Baxter:

'Though this is the first time anybody put it into words.' He touched his hat brim as he added with the trace of a smile at his mouthline: 'Evening to you, Lavinia. How you doing, Billy?'

The tall but thin and frail-looking schoolma'am gripped the upper arm of the retarded man. Billy, who was almost a head shorter than she was, used to be just as slightly built. But regular heavy work out at Trail's End had thickened and hardened his frame. And it was easy for him to jerk free of the woman's hold, lunge across the porch and down the steps. On his acned, slack-mouthed, bulging-eyed face was an expression that alternated rapidly between a beaming grin and something akin to terror.

'Mr Steele . . . Boss . . . It sure is good to see you back where . . . I took real good care of the stock while you . . . But I was told not to go out to the place today and . . .'

He halted alongside Steele's gelding. Clenched and unclenched his hands as if he was having to force himself not to reach up and touch the Virginian. This as he shot several guilty glances back at the doorway, like one of Miss Attwood's students, placed on his honour by her not to do something he so desperately wanted to do. Which, it was plain to see, was to demonstrate his respect, even love, for Steele: and the depth of his dread of what was going to happen.

'Easy, Billy,' Steele placated as he swung down from his saddle. Grinned, and in a gesture of affection punched the simpleton lightly on the shoulder. 'I'm happy to be back, I can tell you.'

He shifted his eyes, which had taken no part in the grin, to look at the frowning woman as she came down off the porch with more decorum than Billy. Added grimly: 'No matter what I've come back to?'

Miss Attwood told him: 'Adam, a couple who claim they are the rightful owners are out at Trail's End.'

Billy started to blurt eagerly: 'Yeah, and then another——'

Steele pushed the reins of the gelding into Billy's hands. Said, hard-toned as he struggled to check his impatience: 'Be grateful if you'll take the horses to the livery for me. Have them fed and watered?'

'I sure will, boss.'

Billy led the animals away and Grout ducked back into the saloon, obviously to sink an unfinished drink. This as Steele swung to the side, to smoothly slide the Colt Hartford from the boot hanging forward on the right of the saddle of the moving gelding.

'What Billy was about to tell you, Steele . . .' Tom Knight drawled from the hallway of the boarding house, before his heavily built wife appeared alongside the narrow-chested, pot-bellied man and snapped: 'What I'm tellin' you is that you ought to mind your own business, Thomas!'

Blanche spared some of the force of her glower for Steele as she reached around her henpecked husband to slam the door.

Steele tightened the grip of his right gloved hand around the frame of the Colt Hartford as he canted the rifle to his shoulder. Then ran the buckskin-covered back of his left hand along his jaw: made a rasping sound on the day's growth of grey and dark red bristles that sprouted across his lower face. While his eyes extended a tacit invitation for the anxious schoolteacher to finish her explanation, now that those who had interrupted her were otherwise engaged.

'You look beat, Adam,' she said with feeling, after studying him from head to toe. Saw the stained and rumpled state of his dark-hued, Western style clothing that looked like it had been slept in more nights than not during the time he was away. 'Perhaps you'd like to talk in the schoolhouse?'

She cast a scowl at the closed door behind her. 'Clean off some of the miles? Sit down on something that isn't moving while I tell you——'

'From what I've heard so far, I don't reckon I have the time for that,' he answered. And looked toward Grout as the liveryman left the saloon to head to where Billy Baxter held the horses out front of the stable. Raised his voice to request: 'Grateful if you'll stable all of them, Harlan. Switch my saddle to a mount I can rent?'

Grout nodded enthusiastically, relishing the prospect of completing the most profitable day for many weeks in his livery business.

Steele said to the schoolteacher then: 'Right here is fine with me.'

She looked like she was about to take issue with him. But after she met and held his determined gaze for a stretched second, allowed she knew him well enough to comply with his wish.

'A couple called Elmer and Lydia Rice came to town on

this morning's stage. Boarded it at Broadwater with just a carpetbag which one of the stage men thought might contain a shotgun. The man said little outside of how much he was looking forward to becoming a part of our community. Which contradicted what his wife, who drinks and is foul mouthed, said in the saloon.'

Miss Attwood scowled at the memory of events she had learned of at second hand. 'They were fighting when they arrived—literally fighting, Adam. He punched and kicked her and she bit him. She said they were arguing because she wants to stay on at Trail's End, and he feels they should sell out.

'Her maiden name was Sanderson, they claim. And although she is only distantly related to the Sandersons who used to have the place, she is the sole heir. They claim.'

'I'm grateful to you,' Steele said absently, watching as the two men herded the horses into the livery. 'They went right on out to the place?'

Miss Attwood nodded, tight lipped. 'They did. Just as soon as the woman had imbibed three whiskeys and a glass of beer and almost attacked Mr Attrill for asking too many questions. While her husband saw to the rent of a pair of saddle horses from Harlan.'

'Thanks again.'

Steele made to go toward the livery as lamplight spilled out through the double doorway.

'There is more, Adam.'

He vented an impatient grunt. Then recalled how Billy Baxter and Tom Knight had been prevented from interjecting additional information. He looked quizzically at the woman.

'This afternoon, a man rode in from the south. A good looking, personable young man: or so those of us who happened to notice him in passing considered.'

She shook her head, annoyed at her own gullibility. Hardened her tone. 'But he turned out to be not what he appeared. He called upon Len Fallows at the law office. To ask directions to Trail's End. Quite reasonably, in view of what happened this morning, the sheriff required to know something about the man and his reasons for going to Trail's End.'

Now the schoolma'am's sharp features expressed the most troubled frown yet. 'He became vicious with Len. Threatened to kill him with his own gun unless . . . Well, Len supplied the directions and then the man knocked him unconscious with a blow to the head. Rode off, on the north trail. Leaving poor Len slumped across his desk, none of us aware of what had happened. Until he recovered sufficiently to stumble to the doorway.

'Thadius Mackay has ordered him to remain in bed for at least twenty-four hours. It was a considerable blow: with Len's own gun!'

Thadius Mackay was the town doctor. Steele recalled the passing thought which had struck him about the lighted bedroom window at the Fallows house. But his mind quickly filled with other considerations and he hardly heard what Lavinia Attwood was telling him now.

'I saw to it that Arlene was advised not to go out to Trail's End. Billy: poor dull-witted Billy . . . Of course, he wanted to rush out and take your part, Adam. I managed to keep him here for supper. You know how he loves good food. But what I'd have done after he had eaten, I just don't know.'

'I'm grateful,' Steele added.

'And I'm so very sorry, Adam,' she replied.

He had made to swing away from her again. To go toward the livery's open doorway. But he paused. Met the intense gaze in her eyes: which expressed more emotion than a woman with her inhibitions was ever likely to put into words.

'Just when everything was starting to look so fine,' she explained. 'So settled. This had to happen.'

'I know what you mean,' the Virginian told her. Once more smiled with just his mouth. 'But, like I've been known to say from time to time: a man has to take the rough with the smooth. And don't some others say nothing that's worth-while ever came easy?'

She replied sorrowfully: 'If the latter were true, Adam, I'd have thought you should have a surfeit of what is worthwhile.'

'I have,' he answered absently as Harlan Grout led a big chestnut gelding out of the stable, his own saddle on the animal's back. Hardened his tone to add: 'And I intend to keep it.'

Miss Attwood's sharp featured face spread with a frown of deep concern as she argued: 'But, Adam... If the Rice couple have legal claim to Trail's End as they maintain, then surely you must step down and allow them to have——'

Steele looked over his left shoulder at her, his dark eyes cold as a winter night as he tightened his grip around the rifle sloped to the right. And the woman was reminded of her afternoon reflections about this man's violent past as he rasped through clenched teeth:

'Isn't possession nine tenths of the law, lady?'

She swallowed hard and reminded him: 'But, Adam, they have possession now!'

He nodded, then showed a mirthless grin as he countered: 'If anyone reckons they can take that piece of land away from me... Well, they just have to be de-ranged.'

5

The Virginian had not too much trouble keeping his mind free of anger, resentment or anxiety as he headed along the timber-flanked, moonlight-dappled north trail astride a fresh horse.

He knew just the bare facts of the day's events in Providence as they related to him and there was no point in dwelling on them. To make himself a victim of the temptation to imagine, based on their flimsy foundation, what the future could hold.

And the impassive expression on his bristled face showed in truth his state of mind as he made the half mile trip from town to the point where the trail to Broadwater and the Providence River curved toward each other. Where he angled on to the spur, forded the river and began to climb the fir-cloaked slope alongside the narrower Timber Creek which tumbled over its rocky bed without white water force now that it was summer.

Perhaps he had to work a little harder at keeping unbidden thoughts from his mind now that he was drawing closer to the spread. Or maybe he kidded himself. For on the steepening slope which rose to the lip of an extensive plateau, the well rested and stable-stale gelding required less rein control to keep him moving at an easy pace through the warm, pine-scented night. Which gave Steele greater opportunity to indulge in feelings better confined to his subconscious. Maybe he had wanted to from the start, while the skittish horse needed so much attention.

But surely he had gone that route too often before? Nowadays he should be through with that kind of thinking:

the kind which could so easily lead him toward a brand of maudlin self-pity that he always had cause to regret. It had happened more times than he cared to recall, during that period of his drifting life while he searched for stability: which it often seemed he was destined never to find. Now he had it, and because of this the danger of indulging in futile anxieties was heightened: now there was little more to be gained and so much—everything—to lose.

A curse made a rasping escape through clenched teeth as he reached the boundary of Trail's End. And a scowl of self anger spread across his earlier impassive face and set hard. An acknowledgement that he had failed: he had begun to envisage losing what he had gained before he knew anything more than the spinster schoolteacher had told him.

But, at least, there was no time to feel sorry for what might happen...

The old gateless posts that used to flank the property entrance had been dug out by Billy and himself. The one on the right, seared with the name SANDERSON, had gone first. Now a boundary fence came in from each side, ending at a fifteen feet high post, spanned at the top by a plank lettered with the name TRAIL'S END in black on a white background.

It was a rule adhered to by Arlene, Billy and Steele that the gate be kept closed at all times. A clear-to-read sign on the top rail of the gate warned visitors: LIVESTOCK—CLOSE THE GATE. Tonight the gate hung open and on this occasion Steele ignored his own rule: rode on to the place without pausing.

As he did so he was disconcerted to feel a burning sensation in his throat, then a tightening of his chest. Recognised the symptoms of rising nausea. But the sensations were gone as soon as he identified their cause. This as he reached the point on the track where he could see for himself stronger evidence than an open gate of the unwelcome visitors to Trail's End.

Beyond the timber there were more than three thousand

acres of rolling country with a fence around them: spread to the north and mostly to the west of this corner of the property. Everything out there looked wonderfully peaceful in the soft moonlight.

Just as the scene closer at hand would have appeared domestically tranquil to a stranger who reined in his mount where Steele did. But such a stranger would not have shown such a coldly angry expression as the Virginian while he surveyed the panorama: raking his glinting-eyed gaze over a piece of land on which he had expended so much time and effort and money.

He was unprepared to even contemplate the premise he was the interloper: that the people occupying Trail's End were, indeed, the rightful owners. And, he allowed, he probably never had been prepared to accept such a premise.

It was five hundred feet from where he had paused to the hard-packed yard bounded by the house, the barn, the corral and one of the two crop fields that flanked the final stretch of track. Over this distance he saw that smoke rose from the chimney at the far end of the longer than it was wide timber and fieldstone house with its front to back pitched roof. Light squared each of the two windows which flanked the centrally placed door, brighter at the further, kitchen end of the one-roomed shack. The milk cow had not yet been taken into the barn from the corral and the chickens still ranged free at this time of night. The double doors of the barn stood open.

'Goddamnit to hell,' Steele growled, forcing his voice low as he ran a gloved palm down the neck of his rented mount. 'Let's go run these squatters off my land.'

But before he could heel the gelding forward, two gunshots exploded. Close together. Separated by a moment filled with the shattering of glass and, indistinct behind this, the cry of a human voice.

Steele did not need to wrench his head around to look toward the sound, for as he spoke his acid-toned intention, his narrow-eyed gaze was already fastened on the more brightly lit of the two windows. Which was the window that was shattered by the blast of the shotgun.

He saw a myriad shards of glass shower out across the yard, to put a pair of hens to clumsy, clucking flight. Then he heard the cry, too fleeting for the tone to be identified as one of fear, pain, anguish or anger. Next the second report as he guessed the second barrel of a double-barrel shotgun was discharged. And a shriek of such high pitch that he was sure it was vented from the throat of a woman.

Just as, from much closer than the house, a man groaned: 'Sonofagoddamnbitch!'

Steele snapped his head around this time. And looked down to his right. Into a patch of brush between the trees and a field in which grew cabbages and potatoes: and a second sowing of salad crops was about ready for harvesting.

He glimpsed a powerful looking frame as it rose up out of the thicket that had been his own hiding place when he first came secretly to Trail's End. Next he was aware of a head of thick, dark-coloured, curly hair. Then a pair of glinting eyes and some gleaming teeth clenched in a scowl.

The man was on him, leaping clear of the ground with both arms curled to grip the Virginian around his waist. Dragged him out of the saddle as the gelding, already spooked by the gunshots and the shattering of the window, was made to rear by this sudden flurry of violent movement close to him.

Steele instinctively reached his right hand for the booted Colt Hartford. But it was knocked down, the arm trapped to his side by the vice-like embrace of the man. Then the two of them were momentarily in mid-air, falling, locked together as the horse bolted away from beneath them.

Both crashed heavily to the ground, Steele winded the worse because of the man who was on top of him, his not inconsiderable weight adding to the force of impact.

The Virginian responded to the pain that jarred his entire body but which did not debilitate him. Knew it was futile to indulge the hurt: knew that the worse the pain, the more he had to fight back before the man increased the agony. Even killed him. In much the same way as he used fear to hone his reflexes in other situations, so now he harnessed pain to give power to the muscles with which he struggled to fight back at the cursing, grunting man who made to follow up his opening advantage.

But the man would not respond in the way Steele expected. Steele brought up his free arm, gloved fist clenched. Felt it slam into something solid. But this was not the jaw for which he had aimed. His fist hurt and he guessed his knuckles had connected with the skull of the curly haired man. Who must have ducked his head as he straddled Steele, crotch pressing down on the Virginian's belly, forcing the base of his spine painfully against the hard ground beneath.

'You're the crazy hick sonofabitch that fixed this lousy place up?' the man rasped.

'Damn right!' Steele forced out through gritted teeth, feeling resentment at being called a hick. He tried again to bring up a fist into the scowling face of the man. Who, he was sure, must be the same one who gave the Providence sheriff such a hard time. Even as the man prepared to avoid the punch and to counter it, the Virginian found himself allowing that, in different circumstances, he might like the look of the personable young man of which Lavinia Attwood had spoken.

Steele felt disorientated. He formulated a curse in his mind. But did not think he voiced it. Realised he was getting light-headed. This as the younger man knocked aside the slow and clumsy roundhouse blow, then easily made Steele helpless. Spreadeagled on the ground, both arms pinioned under kneecaps that felt like they were made of iron.

'Ain't nothin' I can do but this, you poor, hick sonofabitch!' Steele heard rasped from outside his head. That insulting term again.

'It's my place, feller,' Steele felt sure he heard himself speak, very much aloud this time. Maybe he yelled the claim.

'Not anymore it ain't, ' the other voice argued.

Steele tried to launch a punch, then remembered both his

arms were trapped under the legs of the man with the curly hair. Who was free to swing back a clenched fist. Throw it viciously down at the man beneath him as he muttered, with what sounded like genuine feeling in the confused mind of the Virginian:

'Man, I'm real sorry about this, you poor, hick sonofabitch.'

Steele thought he heard himself respond: 'But I reckon this is going to hurt me more than it hurts you, uh?'

6

... *Is going to hurt me more than it hurts you, uh?'* Steele heard somebody shout in a slurred, echoing tone that suggested the voice came from the depths of a deep well or far off along a narrow tunnel.

Another voice promised vehemently.: 'This time you're dead, Steele.' A vaguely familiar voice which triggered recognition of the first speaker: damnit, that had been him!

There was a rumbling buzz of many voices, too many for him to hear anything of what was being said. Then this body of sound faltered to an end as he eased open his eyes, saw a circle of faces peering down at him from far above. As indistinct as the chorus of voices had been.

He recalled a state of disorientation: when he seemed to have hallucinated, after he was badly hurt. Was this part of the same waking nightmare?

He was still down on his back, but not spreadeagled, he was sure. Now behind the heads that surrounded him was a light many times brighter than that of the moon. Which, it came back to him, had illuminated the night sky in front of which had been the man who smashed a fist into his face. Made his jaw hurt worse than the base of his spine on which he landed when he was knocked off his horse.

He began to feel easier in his mind as he remembered the past.

'The murderin' sonofabitch come out of it, has he?' This a woman's voice, clearly heard, unrecognisable.

'Adam?' Soft and concerned, spoken by Lavinia Attwood. And as Steele recognised the schoolteacher he matched a name to another voice. The man who had crowed in triumph of the certain end which awaited him on account of something he knew nothing about.

He allowed his eyelids to close again. While he attempted to recall the circumstances which had surrounded one vividly remembered scene: when he was the helpless victim of the curly haired hard man who claimed he was sorry to be beating up on Steele. But the throbbing pain in the side of his jaw was intensified by the darkness. And the closing of his eyes acted to trigger a renewed barrage of protesting voices: the sound of which gave an even sharper dimension to the hurt.

'Like all of you to shut up for awhile so a feller has time to think,' he growled. Snapped open his eyes and instantly saw clearly, able to recognise his surroundings and most of the people there.

He was on his back on the floor, head toward the front doorway of his house at Trail's End. The light, not looking so dazzlingly bright now, came from the two lamps which were suspended from hooks in the ceiling at either end of the room, both wicks turned high.

The Providence schoolteacher was in the ragged circle of people who peered down at him, one of three women in the group. One of five men was Len Fallows, who had gloated about the Virginian's impending doom.

Just as Miss Attwood's face showed the kind of disquiet that had earlier sounded in her voice, so the lawman expressed the sadistic pleasure that had rung in his tone. Huey Attrill, Ethan Brady, Harlan Grout and the fat, florid-faced Dr Thadius Mackay all looked despondent: in degree ranging from mournful to something like pity.

One of the women was a stranger to Steele. A thick-bodied, fifty-years-old, greying redhead with a pallid complexion and beady eyes which stared down at him with the kind of hatred he would expect only from somebody he had badly wronged.

The third woman was Susannah Lineker, an attractive, willowy blonde of thirty-five who looked her age but often tended to act some twenty years younger than this: particularly when she was anywhere close to Adam Steele. Right now, when their eyes met, she made to say something. But when he looked elsewhere she began to spill tears out of eyes already red-rimmed and swollen from earlier weeping.

In the manner of berating one of her over-reacting younger students, Miss Attwood told Susannah to pull herself together.

Steele had rolled his head to the side. Seeking clues to other pieces of the past he was beginning to fit into place as he recalled everything that had happened to him before the blow to his jaw plunged him suddenly into unfeeling darkness. He saw there was somebody else in the shack he had transformed from a derelict shell into a clean and comfortable home. A silent figure, totally inert beneath a bloodstained blanket. Probably lying where he had fallen close to the shattered window. Having gone down before the second blast from the shotgun.

He saw this blanket-draped form—a man it looked like—not very tall and slightly built, between the legs of Attrill and Brady. Ignored the question he was asked as he rolled his head back the other way, to look toward the sleeping quarters end of the house. In search of the curly haired man who had helped him get himself into this latest mess.

'You hear me, Steele?' The words were spat out like pebbles, which tasted foul in the mouth of Len Fallows. 'Sure you do. You're just faking that you're——'

'The lady who's a stranger to me is Lydia Rice, I reckon?' the Virginian cut in wearily as he straightened his head, peered directly up at the angry sheriff. 'And the corpse under the blanket is what's left of Elmer?'

'As if you didn't friggin' know that!' Lydia Rice challenged, beady eyes blazing.

Susannah Lineker sobbed more loudly.

'I told you to pull yourself together, you stupid woman!' Miss Attwood snapped. Lowered her voice to advise: 'Adam, I feel you should take more time to collect your thoughts before you——'

'I don't see the other one,' Steele interrupted. And felt sufficiently aware of himself and his situation to raise a gloved hand to tentatively explore the left side of his jaw. Only now discovered his hands were bound at the wrists, so realised he had some more recovering to do.

He decided that, as usual with swellings that could not be seen, the bruise on his face could not possibly be as massive as it felt.

'What other one?' Ethan Brady demanded, mopped at his sweat-free face. And Steele was struck by a notion that made him think he was well advanced along the road toward total recovery. The banker was nervous because he was worried about losing the two thousand dollars he had loaned to the Virginian to buy stud horses.

'He's fakin' again, pretendin' his mind's wanderin'!' Lydia Rice accused.

'The one that jumped me and knocked me out,' Steele said, concentrating his attention on the scowling Fallows. 'You know he can do that, sheriff? A curly haired feller?'

'Don't try to get too smart, Steele,' the lawman warned, a sneer in his voice. 'You heard about what happened to me this afternoon, I know that.'

He took the time to glower across the circle at Lavinia Attwood. Who returned his gaze with a fixed stare that forced him to look down at the Virginian again before he would have chosen to do so. Concluded: 'Mrs Rice told me how that hard-nosed drifter came by this afternoon. Looking for work. And right off was sent on his way.'

'So forget about tryin' to sell folks that pack of lies!' Lydia Rice said. Like everyone else, she ignored a choked cry from Susannah and went on: 'You rode up here to the house and wouldn't listen to what Elmer and me told you. You got mad and snatched up Elmer's shotgun. First you blasted out the window, and then you got mad enough to blast Elmer, full in the chest. Would've done the same to me, I figure. If you'd got the gun reloaded fast enough. Before I swung the skillet at you. Laid you out cold. Tied your hands and took off to town for help. There ain't no story you can tell that'll change the truth of what happened. And that's the truth, frig it!'

She glared around the circle.

'Madam, kindly take care with your language!' Miss Attwood said tautly.

'I'll do that, schoolteacher!' Lydia Rice raged. 'If I'm in your place. I'm in mine now and so I'll do as I friggin' well please! And what I'd be pleased for now is for you all to clear outta my house! Take this murderin' sonofabitch with you! So I can get to mournin' my poor Elmer. Go on, get the hell outta here!'

She started to weep, spilling tears down her wan cheeks more copiously than had Susannah Lineker. Then suddenly stopped and, like everyone else, wrenched her head around. As a barrage of gunfire exploded out front of the house. Interspersed with the voice of a man, yelling incoherently. Then the thudding of hooves and the snorting of horses spooked into gallops by the eruption of raucous sound.

As the shooting and the shouting finished, the group around Steele whirled away. Some went toward the unbroken window: even in their confusion they made the conscious decision to stay clear of the corpse beneath the bloodstained blanket. Others lunged to the door as Harlan Grout wrenched it open and yelled, unnecessarily:

'Somebody's run off our horses, damnit!'

Steele folded his back up off the floor, the pain in his spine forcing a groan through his gritted teeth.

Huey Attrill shouted as he turned away from the window: 'It's that lame-brained Billy Baxter, Len!'

'Yes, I saw him, too!' Ethan Brady added, mopping at his face.

Fallows snapped as he stepped out of the doorway: 'You women, watch the prisoner!'

Then he halted: glared over the threshold to meet and hold the quizzical gaze Steele directed at him. But had to wait for Attrill, Brady and the obese Mackay to hurry outside before he was able to reach back and thrust his Frontier Colt through the doorway. Lydia Rice made a grab for it, but

Fallows snatched it away from her. Growled against the diminishing sound of racing hooves and the cursing voices of the men trying to catch the runaways:

'No, ma'am! You'd likely kill him if he even looked at you the wrong way. He's got to stand legal trial.' He eyed the schoolteacher gravely. 'I'm counting on you, Lavinia. As one of our most respected citizens.'

Miss Attwood hesitated for a second. Then she took the revolver. And for a further second, as the sheriff turned and began to run in the wake of the other men, seemed by her expression and how she gripped the Colt, like she did not know how to handle it: nor had any inclination to learn. Then, when she glimpsed the contemptuous smile which twisted the lips of Lydia Rice, she took a double-handed grip on the butt, thumbed back the hammer and curled both forefingers to the trigger. By tucking her elbows into her hips and bending them, raised the Colt and held it vertically alongside her left cheek, pointed at the ceiling. Threatening no-one but maintaining a menacing attitude that immediately wiped the scorn off the pale face of the new widow.

She started to explain: 'You know, Adam, that I would not have wished——'

'What the hell you lookin' at?' Lydia Rice snarled at Susannah Lineker.

And the demand drew the attention of the schoolteacher and the Virginian toward the tearstained face of the slender blonde. Saw she was staring fixedly at the rear corner of the shack at the kitchen end.

'Susannah?' Steele's tone was cold as his head snapped back and forth, his gaze switching from the woman to the rear door of the shack and back again.

'Really, Miss Lineker!' Lavinia Attwood accused impatiently. 'Have you been struck dumb?'

'The door!' Susannah pointed to it. 'Just as the men were leaving! I'm certain I saw it open and close. I know——'

She broke off with a sharp intake of breath. And Miss Attwood, Steele and Lydia Rice all looked at the door with the same kind of unblinking intensity as Susannah. All, too, sharing much the same kind of fear of the unknown. But unlike the women, Steele was not affected by temporary paralysis as the door cracked open and the gap slowly widened. For he used the prospect of imminent death—should the curly headed man step into sight with gun blazing—to transcend pain, oil the stiffness out of muscles unused for a long time. Tensed himself for a fast move. To spring up, get the hands of his bound wrists on the revolver still aimed uselessly at the ceiling in the grip of the schoolteacher. Surely certain to die in the attempt if this was what was intended by the man opening the door. But determined to make the try.

But it was not a man! A woman: a Negress of past sixty with a round, shiny face beneath a mop of jet black hair curled far more tightly than that of the man he expected. A short, heavily built woman named Arlene Forrester who looked completely unafraid as she levelled Steele's Colt Hartford from her right hip. Aimed it at the schoolteacher and looked and sounded regretful but determined as she warned:

'I ain't sure I can hit anyone if I have to pull this trigger, Miss Attwood, ma'am. And I just knows the good Lord won't never forgive me for the sin of shootin' somebody. Just as I knows for sure I'll try to shoot you if you try to keep Mr Steele from gettin' up off the floor. Comin' out here to where his horse is ready and waitin' for him.'

The moment he saw it was the familiar bulky form of Arlene at the door, Steele felt himself a fool for experiencing fear it would be somebody else. Billy Baxter did not possess the wits to stage the diversion with the spooked horses without being told what to do. But he would know better than to follow such instructions from a stranger.

He brought up his knees, so he could use his heels to work himself backwards. Out from between Lydia Rice on one side of him and Miss Attwood and Susannah on the other. Was irritated at how he had been weakened by the strain of gathering himself for a fast move that had proved unnecessary: that he should have realised was unnecessary!

He believed the black woman meant every word she said. He also believed that, should Lavinia Attwood make up her mind to carry out the duty entrusted to her, she would do whatever she felt had to be done.

If lead started to fly from guns in the hands of two women not overly familiar with firearms . . .

Arlene said with feeling, without allowing her attention to wander from the rigidly erect schoolteacher to the painfully moving Steele: 'I'm sorry, Miss Attwood, ma'am. Truly I am.'

Susannah Lineker gasped: 'Oh, my goodness gracious.'

Lydia Rice challenged sneeringly: 'You surely ain't gonna let a fat nigger cow give you orders?'

At the front of the house, far off beyond the corral out across the grazing meadows, the distant voices of men predominated over the thudding of hooves now the horses had galloped out of earshot or slowed from bolts. Closer, in the yard, a horse whinnied, and Steele guessed this was the gelding hitched to Doc Mackay's phaeton, the braked wheels of the rig having prevented the animal from covering more than a few feet when the saddle horses raced off. Out back, not far from the open doorway where Arlene stood, another horse scraped impatiently at the ground with a hoof. Further back, water trickled down Timber Creek toward its confluence with the Providence River.

Steele was aware of these sounds during the two stretched seconds that elapsed after Lydia Rice's words brought a tense silence to the interior of the shack. Then Lavina Attwood said gravely:

'One man already lies dead in this house. I see no point in risking other lives. You may leave, Adam.'

Steele half rose, paused to reach through the slit in the outside seam of his right pants leg and drew the knife from the boot sheath. Then came fully upright. Used the knife first as a menacing weapon while he circled behind Lydia Rice and went toward the rear door, watching the three women near the front door. Saw the schoolteacher stared fixedly into space, while Lydia Rice glowered at him and Susannah eyed him with her little-girl-lost expression, fighting the threat of more tears.

Close to Arlene, he saw in her eyes and from the way fine beads of sweat clung to her shiny skin the kind of strain she was under to maintain the façade of calmness while just beneath the surface she was terrified almost out of her wits.

'I'm real grateful to you and Billy,' he told her in low tones, reached with his empty hand to grasp the barrel of his rifle. Shifted his gaze between her face and the knife clutched in his other hand.

She took the knife and began to cut through the cord that tied his wrists. Said, with a meaningful look toward the other women as the bonds parted: 'We knows you didn't do no killin' here, Mr Steele, sir. Not the murderin' kind, anyhow.'

'I didn't do any kind, Arlene,' he assured her as he stooped to return the knife to its sheath.

'I'm counting on you to prove that, Adam,' Miss Attwood said coldly as her gaze remained fixed on a faraway scene painted on the backdrop of the wall above the fireplace. 'If you do not, I have made a sadly wrong decision here. It would have been better to risk a further tragedy, not betray the trust of Len Fallows, than to set a murderer free.'

The depth of feeling expressed by the tall, elegant spinster was sufficient to draw the fixed attention of everyone in the room. Then she was through, and it was Lydia Rice who did not know this pillar of Providence society who was first to break the spell. With good reason not to see the Virginian turned loose, she made the move to check his escape. Vented an enraged snarl and launched herself toward Miss Attwood, both hands clawed to grab for the gun still aimed at the ceiling.

The schoolteacher was still lost in a mental morass of self-reproach and Steele had just a one-handed grip on the Colt Hartford, around the muzzle end of the barrel.

Arlene shrieked: 'Miss Attwood, watch out!'

At a higher pitch, Susannah Lineker yelled: 'Oh, no you don't!'

And flung herself at Lydia Rice, both her arms flailing like the sails of a windmill. More by luck than intended design, one of her clenched hands caught the widow hard under the jaw. Stopped her in her tracks, held rigidly erect for a second, before she was sent sprawling out on her back. Unconscious as she fell, for when she hit the floor her head slammed into the resilient belly of her recently dead husband beneath the bloodstained blanket.

Susannah, her face a mask of guilty shock, brought her damaging fist to her mouth and bit hard on the side of the forefinger as she stared down with wide eyes at the raggedly breathing woman spread before her.

Arlene urged: 'Mr Steele, sir, best you beat it now.'

Lavinia Attwood jolted free of the numbing effect of doubt. Swept her rapidly blinking eyes from the senseless widow, to the shocked Susannah, then the nervous black woman and the impassive Virginian at the rear doorway. Eased the revolver hammer carefully forward as she brought the weapon down. Let go with one hand so that the gun hung in a loose grip at her side, aimed at the floor.

'Yes, do go, Adam,' she agreed tautly. Paused in a listening attitude, to ensure that the quiet within the house was no longer interrupted by the far off sounds of angry men and running horses. 'Go quickly. And do what you have to do quickly, please. I just hope our trust in you is not misplaced.'

She looked ashamed, but whether at what she was doing or for doubting the Virginian it was impossible to tell. Then she was in total command of herself again, when Susannah caught her breath, as if about to sob, and the schoolteacher snapped at her:

'Do be quiet, woman!' Then to Steele: 'God, hurry up and go!'

Arlene urged breathlessly: 'Good Lord, yes!'

Steele said grimly as he swung toward the rear door: 'I'm only a mere mortal, ladies.' Then he managed a brief sardonic half smile as he glanced back over his shoulder to conclude: 'Never have been able to perform miracles. And I can't even guess how long the impossible's going to take.'

7

Billy Baxter had charge of the rented chestnut gelding. He held the bridle with one hand while in the other he clutched the Colt revolver Steele recognised as the weapon customarily kept in the barn.

The slow-witted man was beaming, obviously bursting to blurt out his own account of the part he played in the scheme to set the Virginian free.

'You did real fine, Billy,' Steele congratulated him as he slid the rifle in the boot and took up the gelding's reins. 'I'm grateful.'

Not for the first time it was demonstrated that Billy paid more respectful heed to what Arlene Forrester told him than he did to anyone else. For he remained tight-lipped, although his eyes continued to gleam with pleasure, as he looked toward the doorway. As the black woman spoke for him.

'Billy knows he did good and how much you appreciates it, sir. And he knows, too, he has to face up to the sheriff and some other townsfolk bein' mad at him, just like they'll be at me. Come on inside, Billy.'

The mentally retarded man pulled a face that suggested he was more unhappy at having to stay with the women than afraid of the trouble he would be in when the men returned with their horses he had scattered. But he grinned in response to the wink the Virginian gave him as he backed away from the horse, turned, and stumbled over the threshold when he first saw the scene inside the house.

Probably, Steele reflected as he swung up into the saddle, Billy was not too bothered by the blanket-draped corpse or the prostrate woman. More likely it was the sight of Lavinia Attwood: certainly children with a true age of six or seven were made nervous by their schoolteacher in a bleak frame of mind.

'Ma'am . . . I . . . I only d-d-done what I——' he started to stutter.

'It's all right, Billy,' Miss Attwood reassured him, her kindly tone just a little strained.

Steele's back hurt as he settled into the saddle on the blind side of the house to the men who must now surely be returning with their captured horses. But it was a level of discomfort he was prepared to endure in the circumstances.

'Sir!' Arlene called anxiously as she came away from the doorway. Cast a furtive look over her shoulder as he eyed her expectantly. Lowered her voice to a whisper to continue: 'Ain't no doubt we can trust Miss Attwood and the Lineker woman I figures, Mr Steele. But Billy might let it slip, the way he is.' She beckoned for him to lean down, put his head close to her face. 'Ain't much else anyone can do to lend a hand. Except, Tom Knight, he's waitin' to let you into the boardin' house. If you wants a place to stay while you're——'

'Arlene, I don't reckon I'll ever be able to repay all I'm beholden to you for,' he cut in, pitching his voice at the same low level. Made to touch the brim of his hat before he recalled the Stetson was missing. Had probably been knocked off during his struggles with the curly haired man.

'To Billy you're near enough a Pa, Mr Steele,' she hurried to get said when hooves were heard, muffled on the lush grassland, but rising in volume as the men neared the front of the house. 'And I don't reckon I've even got started to repay you for what you done for Rosebud and her baby. Now, you better be on your way, sir. And good luck to you.'

She started back for the house, where Lydia Rice could be heard cursing back to angry consciousness. And Steele tugged on his reins to head the gelding into and over the slow-running creek. Was on the far bank and hidden in the moon-shadowed timber before the rear door of the shack closed and blocked off the wedge of lamplight. This as cantering horses were reined down to a walk as they were ridden off the pastureland and their hooves thudded on the hard-packed dirt of the yard.

For perhaps two minutes then, Steele held his mount to a cautious walk. To guard against laming the animal as he rode through the near pitch dark, potentially dangerous timber: the slow pace also acting to keep down the sounds of his escape, so they would not carry back to the men he could hear dismounting in the yard. During this time he was concerned only with avoiding these immediate dangers.

Then he was relatively safe, able to angle through the cover of the trees to reach the track that became the spur trail beyond the still open gateway at the property line. He was now beyond earshot of the house and he asked for a faster pace: galloped the gelding down to where the spur forded the river and joined the Broadwater to Providence trail, the animal as eager for the exercise as he had been earlier. And now Steele gave thought to the visual evidence he was leaving for his pursuers.

At the junction of the spur and the main trail he reined the hardly stretched gelding to a halt. Gently stroked the animal's neck as he listened to their breathing and the rippling of moving water. Heard no other sounds, so perhaps the group at the house were still trading angry talk and bitter recriminations. Or maybe a careful investigation was being made to determine in which direction Steele had gone.

He considered turning his horse northward toward Broadwater: but not as the first step toward fugitive flight and the abandonment of all he had worked for over the past year and a half. Just to lay the start of a token false trail that could delay Fallows and the others. But he quickly discarded this idea.

Enough people now knew him well enough to be certain he would not give up so easily: start out on another series of long and gruelling trails that might someplace stop where he had a chance to re-establish himself in similar circumstances to those at Trail's End.

Even if nobody else thought along such a line, Lavinia Attwood would. The schoolteacher, smarting at having been forced to compromise her principles, would convince Len Fallows the Virginian would never again become a drifting saddletramp. He would take up the opportunity he had been given to prove he did not blast Elmer Rice to death.

He could not achieve this from a distance. Maybe he would go to Broadwater, but only to check on how the Rices had got there to board the stage for Providence.

Steele tugged on his reins to head his mount south, on the trail that curved away from the river toward the town named for it. Leaving tracks which an inexperienced lawman like Fallows and a bunch of small town men and women might or might not spot on such a well-used stretch of trail.

Even if they did take the trouble to look for the tracks and follow them, it was likely they would be persuaded to think the same as if he had laid a false trail north. He was heading south in search of information on the curly haired stranger who had ridden in from that direction. The man he claimed had knocked him out rather than Lydia Rice.

Or, if he was simply going no further south than Providence . . ? Well, everyone in the posse-like group, plus the entire population of the community, knew the area better than he did. And more citizens were likely to turn him in than help him if he showed himself.

Such lines of thought came and went from his mind as he galloped three quarters of the half mile distance to town from the intersection of the main trail and the Timber Creek spur. None of them inspired him with confidence, but at least the uncertainties about the future helped to keep his mind off present aches and pains.

He reined to a halt, dismounted and removed his saddle and gear. As he did so, he listened again for sounds in the night. But except for his own and the gelding's breathing and some small, scurrying noises of creatures in the timber, the silence would have been absolute.

Then, after a sharp word of command and an open-handed slap on the rump, the hooves of the chestnut gelding at a gallop blotted out all other sounds as the horse made for town. Either to run on to and across the square and off along Main Street or, more likely, to angle toward Grout's Livery which was his home.

Steele cut into the trees to the east of the trail. Followed a wide, curving route that in ten minutes or so brought him, wearied by the weight of his saddle and bedroll and hurting sharply at the base of his spine, to the area out back of the boarding house and the neighbouring livery stable.

The town was quiet and there was no atmosphere of tension in back of the country peace. It was invariably quiet at this time of night as far as he knew: he seldom had occasion to be in Providence outside of the business hours of the stores and bank.

Unless trouble had erupted here. Trouble that always seemed to be laid at his door. Tonight, there was no trouble in Providence: it was all happening out at Trail's End. Some local folks had chosen to go out there, along with Len Fallows whose job it was to handle trouble. There would be no news until they returned, and so the town waited quietly.

Whatever disturbance the loose horse had caused was now ended. Or maybe there had been no disturbance, outside of the clop of slow moving hooves as the gelding came on to the square. The good citizens of Providence electing not to involve themselves, even to the extent of satisfying their curiosity, until the sheriff and the others got back. Back from the scene of this latest violence triggered by the decision of Adam Steele to put down roots at the old Sanderson place.

He shook his head sharply and grimaced. Angry at himself for the sense of frustration that caused him to feel so bitter toward his fellow citizens. It was understandable that not too many of them considered his problems their problems.

Now, as he lowered his gear to the ground and leaned gratefully against the side fence of the livery's corral, breathing deeply and wiping sweat from his bristled face, he took the time to reflect upon the most intriguing factor of his escape. The revelation by Arlene that there was safe refuge at the Providence boarding house. A business run primarily by the domineering Blanche Knight who, he had always considered, had little more regard for him than did Len Fallows.

But Arlene had, of course, specifically said it was Tom Knight who offered the room. A man who invariably came off second best to his wife in any dispute. So this could be a case of the henpecked husband making a stand for entirely selfish personal reasons. Having nothing to do with a belief in Steele's innocence. Nor out of any liking for the Virginian—Knight had never been noticeably for him since the town became unequally divided in its views about the drifter who chose to remain in the Providence River Valley. But, then again, neither had he been particularly against Steele.

He was a fence-sitter on every issue. So at least Steele could be sure Tom Knight would not be committed enough to be a party to a double cross.

Something else about Tom Knight, though. Were it not that Blanche kept him on such a tight rein, he would run Harlan Grout a close second for the title of most frequent customer of Harry Krim at the Golden Gate. So maybe Knight had been bolstered by Dutch courage when he made the offer to Arlene. He could now be stone cold sober, regretting his words. Hell, he might even have forgotten.

There was just one way to find out. And after a pause by the corral fence of no more than a minute, Steele moved to put this into effect. Hefted his gear off the ground and surveyed the rear of the two storey frame house, its six windows all darkened.

The livery stable and the bank were also in total darkness. While just a glimmer of light showed at a draped rear window of the stage depot, in a room of the building's living quarters shared by Joanne Morrison and her son, Michael.

He was about to fist a hand around the knob when the rear door of the boarding house folded away from him and he tensed to react. The earlier notion about an unlikely double cross filled his mind. Then Tom Knight's voice growled out of the darkness:

'Hell, Steele, I was wonderin' how long you was gonna hang around out there. Lookin' at the moon or whatever.'

Steele knew, within a moment of the door swinging open, that Tom Knight was not drunk. Then the round face with its small eyes and blue-veined nose came into view and he decided the man was afraid.

He felt his senses were heightened by the combination of events that had happened so fast since he rode into Providence earlier this evening. Detected something was wrong. Then learned from Lavinia Attwood exactly what was amiss. Let himself be jumped by the curly haired man. Was knocked unconscious. Came out of it to find himself accused of blasting a man to death. A series of events which, if carried to its end of a trial in a court of law—as Len Fallows had gloated he intended—signalled at best the loss of the dream he had turned into a reality: at worst, death by hanging.

'You're as sober as I am, feller,' Steele said, and had voiced the words before he knew he was speaking aloud the opinion.

Knight showed a grin that was just a little strained as he beckoned for his visitor to enter. Countered: 'And you never killed the guy whose wife's laid claim to the old Sanderson place.'

His voice was more strained than his expression. And as soon as Steele was in the house, Knight sagged back against the hallway wall and growled:

'Hell, I sure could use a snort now! Let's get to the room I got fixed for you, uh?'

He started along the hallway that ran through the centre of the house from the front to the back. There was a lighted room with a part-open door at the front on the right. Across from the dining room where Steele had once eaten supper as a guest of Lavinia Attwood. But it was not this private sitting room of the Knights that was their destination.

He followed the man up a narrow staircase that made a turn, then another and got even narrower. And now Steele felt his senses were numbed in the wake of that strange sharpness of mind which had gripped him a few seconds earlier. He felt more deeply tired than he could ever remember. His back throbbed and the swelling on his jaw seemed, to his mind, to have doubled the size of his lower face.

Twice he stumbled, then heard Tom Knight giving him instructions: warning him of a turn, when a step was unusually high, or a piece of carpet was frayed. It seemed to Steele that Knight was whispering, his voice forced low to guard against being overheard by somebody. And the Virginian visualised the sudden appearance of Blanche Knight, wide as she was tall, the woman's fleshy face a mask of rage as she roared at her husband for acting against her wishes. Then screamed to the world that there was a murderer in her house.

They reached the top of the stairway and Knight pushed open a door and announced:

'Your room, sir.'

He executed a bow, grinning to demonstrate it was not meant as a gesture of mockery.

And Steele found himself sharply aware of himself and his circumstances again—how he was responding to them. He was close to exhaustion at the end of a very long day which had taken more out of him than he had realised until now. Tom Knight was not whispering. It just seemed to Steele, whose head felt like it was filled with cotton waste, that the man's voice came from a long way off.

'Shit, you look like death, mister,' the pot-bellied, narrow-chested man said, shocked. 'I oughta have give you a hand, damn it!'

He took the saddle and gear off Steele who felt relieved of a mental as well as a physical burden. Saw quite clearly the room into which he stepped at a nod from Knight. An attic, illuminated by the moon that shafted in through two skylights in the east-facing slope of the roof. Used as a store, stacked with crates and cartons and pieces of old or broken furniture: smelling musty.

'I'm grateful, feller,' he said and lowered himself on to a lopsided sofa that was lumpy and spilling its stuffing through a tear. But it felt wonderfully comfortable to him and he recalled what Lavinia Attwood invited. Out front of this very building. When she suggested they go talk in the schoolhouse while he sat on something that was not moving. A lifetime ago, it seemed.

'... soon as I saw the horse come trottin' into town,' Knight was saying. 'I figured you wouldn't be far behind. Me and Harry Krim captured him and put him back in Harlan's stable where he belongs. Don't know if you planned it as a sign to me, but it's what I took it for.'

'I didn't, feller,' Steele replied wearily, leaning the back of his head against the high back of the broken down sofa as he closed his eyes. 'I wasn't thinking too clearly. Whatever, I'm grateful.'

'Recognised it as the horse Harlan rented you.'

'Sure. Something's wrong, Knight?'

'That's for damn sure. Name of Curly.'

The name came and went through Steele's mind and he knew it was important he should have got a grip on it, but did not. Because his still unclear thinking was fastened on something else. A whole lot of things, but one flipped out of the confusion to the forefront of his mind.

'Where's your wife? That's what's wrong, feller.'

'Gone to Broadwater, ain't that beautiful?' Knight answered in a delighted tone. This as he straightened from setting down Steele's gear on the narrow floor of the attic which was boarded only below the ridge of the roof, for the width of the house but just some fifteen feet across from back to front.

'Left me in charge, on account of she didn't figure it mattered. Since the only roomer we got is the schoolteacher and she's near enough like one of the family. But now we got us a new roomer, uh?'

'You let me know how much it'll cost and I'll——'

'Blanche handles the cash, Steele!' he cut in sharply. 'And she ain't here. You can be here for as long as that sister of hers takes to drop the latest baby she's expectin'. The Marlows took Blanche up to Broadwater not so long after you left to go out to your place.

'She reckoned as how I'd drink myself stupid in Harry's place soon as she went. Got to allow, I was startin' in on that, until that Rice female showed up and told what happened out at your place. And Len Fallows and some others hot-footed it out there, Len figurin' to collar you for the killin'.'

The name Curly came into Steele's mind again. And went. Then he felt the need to question Knight on the finer details of the account he was giving. But, most powerful of all was the desire, near irresistible despite everything else, for sleep.

Knight pressed on eagerly: 'Well, soon as I heard the nigger woman planned to get you loose, I figured to lend a hand. Show folks around here—especially Blanche, that's for sure—I ain't just the no-account drunk that I'm all the time took for.'

'Real glad you made that decision,' Steele heard himself answer. Now even his own voice sounded to him like it was coming from far away.

'Come to think of it,' Knight said thoughtfully, and although Steele was unaware of it, the man's manner was actually distant now as his mind drifted away from the moonlit attic cloyed with the stale air of many hot days. 'It's the first damn decision on anything important that I've made in so long I can't recall.'

He looked expectantly at Steele, seeking a response. But thought he had drifted into sleep until, eyes still closed, the Virginian offered:

'Yeah, feller. It sometimes happens people take more of a hand in running our lives than we realise. Until we take the time to figure it out.'

'Damn right!' Knight agreed vehemently. 'And unless we're real careful, life can pass us by and . . . Shit, *I've* only got myself to blame. Most of the time. Hell, I came west to see the elephant, like a whole lot of others. You recall that expression folks used to use? See the elephant? When they started to roll on the wagon trains, way back?'

'I've heard it,' Steele said, experiencing a comfortable warmth and sleepiness. Something like he had felt often in the past year and a half. Out at Trail's End. When he sat in his chair, reading or thinking or simply sitting at the end of a long and satisfying day: looking forward to just such another day tomorrow. When it was much easier to drop off into sleep in the chair, than to take the time and trouble to undress and go to bed.

Now, though, the circumstances were entirely different. He was not at Trail's End. It had not been a good day. And tomorrow, or even tonight, his situation was likely to get worse.

'Trouble was,' Tom Knight growled, 'when I got to see the damn elephant it was pink! And after that I started to see blue mosquitoes and green spiders!'

'Know the feeling,' Steele said, briefly recalling the massive orgy of drink he had embarked upon in a Sonora cantina long ago.

'You do?' Knight was incredulous for, like everyone else in Providence, he knew the Virginian was not a drinking man. Never took anything stronger than a cup of coffee in the Golden Gate. Then he did a double-take at Steele. Decided the man was too groggy to be sure of what he was saying: merely responded with what he thought was an appropriate answer to anything said to him.

'Well, I'll leave you to rest up some now,' Knight said as he went to the door. 'Like I say, you don't have to worry about stayin' here, long as Blanche is with her sister. Except when the schoolteacher's around the place, of course. You'll have to be quiet then. Although I don't guess Miss Attwood would turn you in, uh?'

'I wouldn't like to put her in the position she has to decide,' Steele said. 'Thanks again. I'll try not to be any more trouble to you.'

'Pleasure for me to take the trouble, Steele,' came the forceful reply. 'Hell, I could die tonight and I'll die happier than before. Knowin' I've done somethin' I'd made up my own mind to do.'

'Good.'

Knight scowled. 'Damnit, I'm a fool! Talkin' about dyin' and all, the way things are.'

'Forget it,' Steele assured, turned and swung his feet up on the sofa, to stretch out along it, his head at the end beyond the reach of the moonlight which angled in through the skylights. 'Been times I reckon I've been a lot closer to death than now.'

Knight shuddered and answered: 'Yeah, so let's not think about it, uh?'

'Thinking about dying doesn't bother me,' Steele was not sure if he replied or simply thought. And perhaps he smiled wryly as he added: 'But it's the last thing I want to do.'

8

Steele came awake to brilliant sunlight that smarted his eyes. But they did not hurt so much as his throat, which felt searingly desert dry. Then the worst pain of all jolted along the length of his spine as he tried to get out of bed.

Which was not a bed, he remembered. As the events which led to him waking in the attic of the Providence boarding house flooded into his mind. Tumbling over each other, like they were struggling wilfully to be first in line for consideration.

He closed his eyes and lay still for what he thought was several seconds: there was no yardstick against which to measure the passage of time in the darkness. Nor any inclination to try to make the calculation.

His mind was clear, filled with memories in the correct chronology as he concentrated on the present. Listening to what was happening out beyond the darkness of his closed eyelids and the locked-in capsule of his mind crowded with images of the immediate past. Refused to contemplate the possibility that maybe what he thought of as the immediate past was longer ago than a few hours. Spanned much more than a night between when he was shown into a musty attic and the next dawn.

The alternative did not bear thinking about: a whole series of forgotten hours mounting into days and nights not registered by his conscious mind. Or temporarily blocked out at this present newly awakened stage.

The town was quiet. Assuming he was still in the Knights' rooming house—not the condemned cell of a penitentiary. Hell, this was crazy! He snapped open his eyes again. And remembered to raise just his head so the potential for pain latent in his lower spine did not flare. Felt his jaw hurt a little now: as a smile spread across his face to re-awaken the familiar lesser discomfort of the bruise from where Curly slugged him.

Curly: it was a name known to Tom Knight. Or at least there was something lodged in Steele's mind that made it seem Knight had spoken of Curly with a capital *C*. Not just of an indefinite curly haired man who had leapt out of the thicket of brushwood just as Elmer Rice was getting blasted to death . . .

He was going too fast.

He had seen he was in the attic of the Knight boarding house in Providence. And since the sun that shafted into the room, not directly into his face, came through the two skylights he recalled were in the eastern slope of the pitched roof, it was morning. Early morning, because of the angle the sunlight came in. Early morning, too, because the town was so quiet: the only sounds coming from the timber that was spread on all sides of where he now lay. Birds reaching the end of their dawn chorus.

Then he heard regular creaking sounds from closer at hand than the trees which enclosed the town square. Inside the house. Slow, furtive footfalls on stairs. Somebody who did not want the sounds of his or her approach to be overheard.

Steele, now knowing exactly where the sources of his discomforts were located, was able to rise up from the lumpy, split, stuffing-spilling sofa and to swing his feet to the floor with relative ease. There was a dull ringing in his head, but his back didn't really hurt so much now he knew to move without haste.

He was able to reach out and slide the Colt Hartford from the boot on his saddle without shifting from the sofa. Sure in his own mind he had made little noise, and the steady advance of footfalls on the stairs was proof of this. The man or woman—Tom or Blanche Knight . . ? Lavinia Attwood or

Len Fallows..? Billy or Arlene..?—came closer without hesitation.

There was time to check that the chambers of the Colt Hartford were still fully loaded. Time to aim the rifle toward the door at the end of the boarded area of the attic as he hooked a gloved thumb over the hammer. Time to sit in this muscle-aching attitude for stretched seconds before the knob turned and the door swung inwards. Time to become as tense as he had been last night when the back door of the boarding house was opened: and he failed to smell liquor on a man's breath.

On this occasion smelled a welcome aroma of freshly brewed coffee. Just before he recognised the familiar broad-shouldered and pot-bellied frame and the round face and red hair of Harry Krim. The saloonkeeper not wearing his usual leather waist apron but otherwise looking as he generally did to Steele. Even to the extent that he carried a tray on which stood a pot of coffee and a large china mug.

Krim froze and caught his breath, his eyes widening in fear as he looked at the aimed rifle.

'I'm sorry,' Steele said. And a bone cracked in his arm as his tension eased and he quickly turned, uncaring about the discomfort in his back as he slid the rifle into the boot. 'I didn't know who you were.'

'It's okay, Mr Steele,' Krim rasped and vented a whistling sigh of relief. Looked to be on the point of having his legs give way beneath him. But after he took a moment to recover he stepped over the threshold, a hangdog expression on his face. 'I shoulda knocked on the door, I guess. Waited to find out if you was awake.' Now he shrugged and almost tipped the pot and mug off the tilting tray. 'I figured you could use some coffee? Wasn't sure about eatin'. Maybe Tom'll see to that when he wakes up?'

'The coffee smells like it's all I want in the world right now.'

Krim advanced fully into the attic and did not close the door behind him. Stooped and set the tray on the floor, grimaced as he straightened.

'Something?' Steele asked, and found the aches were almost gone now that he had started to move this way and that after a night of apparently total inertia on the sofa. Or maybe it was just the appetising fragrance of the coffee soon to be coursing down his throat and into his belly: dulling his awareness to everything else as he leaned down to pour the inky black, aromatically steaming liquid into the big mug.

'It'll take Tom a little while to wake up, Mr Steele,' Krim answered. He could not hold the Virginian's steady gaze and it was plain he was merely embarrassed at having to apologise for Knight. 'He sank better than a bottle of rye last night. After you was safe up here. His nerves were pretty well shot, I guess.'

'I'm sure not about to criticise him for that, feller,' Steele answered. Held the mug in both hands, which shook until he had taken some sips of its contents, which acted to settle his own nerves.

'Course, it did serve another purpose,' the saloonkeeper hurried to expand his excuse for Knight. 'Though I don't guess Tom'd claim that was part of what he was aimin' for.

'The folks that came back from out at the old Sanderson... Trail's End... Your place... They didn't expect Tom to be anythin' else except drunk. With Blanche bein' up with her sister in Broadwater.'

Steele asked: 'You have the time to fill me in on what's happened?'

Krim had not shaved and he rasped the back of a hand along his bristled jaw. Probably he had not washed up, either, since he got out of bed and made the coffee to bring to the attic of the rooming house. He looked uneasy, but not afraid. Then he shrugged and dragged across a wooden crate. Sat on it before he answered:

'It's only just about six, Mr Steele. Won't nobody want me 'til nine at least. Maybe ten even. Harlan, he put away more than a couple of quick ones before he bedded down last night. He sure won't be up early today.'

'You want to close the door?'

'It don't matter. If you're concerned about wakin' Miss Attwood, that is. She didn't stay in her room her last night. You know how she can be? Her bein' a spinster and all? Didn't take to the idea of bein' alone in the house with a man: with Blanche gone. Little she knew there were two men here, uh?'

He experimented with a brief grin, but his heart was not in it. And Steele did not appear to be paying attention to him: like the Virginian needed all his concentration to drink the coffee. But then Steele proved he was not totally detached from what Krim was saying, when he suggested:

'Stayed over at the schoolhouse?'

Miss Attwood had improvised the desk in her study into a bed on another occasion when she considered it was unwise to sleep in her room at the boarding house.

'Right, Mr Steele.'

'Truly would be most grateful if you'd tell me what happened after I left town yesterday, feller?'

Krim did so, his account of events quickly becoming fluid after a faltering start.

Soon after Steele rode out of Providence following the exchange with Lavinia Attwood, the Reverend Joseph Marlow and his wife called as arranged earlier at the Knight boarding house to take Blanche to stay with her younger sister who was in confinement at Broadwater.

Then the evening routine of the community returned to uneventful normal until, something over an hour later, Lydia Rice galloped her horse on to the square, yelling for the sheriff and that there had been a murder.

Len Fallows was at home, still nursing his head from getting slugged by the stranger in the afternoon. So Mrs Rice went into the Golden Gate for a calming drink. And Billy Baxter, who was staying at the livery in the absence of the Marlows—self-importantly keeping an eye on Steele's horses—was sent on the run to bring the lawman.

Meantime, Lydia Rice gave her account of violent events

out at Trail's End to the men gathered in the saloon and the cluster of men and women crowded at the doorway. Her version was as Steele had heard it out at his house. He had ridden up to the place, ordered the Rices off the property and gone crazy when they refused to go. So he had snatched up Elmer Rice's shotgun, blasted out the window as a warning, then killed the man when he protested. Was knocked unconscious by Lydia with a skillet while he was in process of reloading with the intent to kill her.

Among those listening at the door of the Golden Gate was Lavinia Attwood: and Arlene Forrester who had been on her way from her shack to the livery to see that Billy was all right in the stable.

Fallows showed up, listened to what Lydia Rice told him, then deputised the two men standing closest to him to help bring in Steele. Who, the Rice woman said, she had trussed up and left, still unconscious, at the house.

Thus had Ethan Brady and Harlan Grout been pressed into becoming deputies. Huey Attrill went as a newspaper-man to get an on-the-spot story. Miss Attwood insisted upon accompanying the men to see that Steele was not mistreated in the circumstances. She it was who saw Doc Mackay in the saloon and shamed him into joining the group in the event Steele needed medical treatment for his injuries. Susannah Lineker, who arrived late on the scene, was allowed to go providing she quit her weeping claims that Adam Steele could not have killed anybody.

When this group had left, the town once again returned quickly to normal: after the gossiping groups soon talked the known details about the subject into the ground. Just Krim and Knight remained in the Golden Gate.

Knight, who would have been expected to get roaring drunk in the absence of his wife, irrespective of side issues, was strangely quiet. And got started on a disjointed tale about a man called Curly he had come across in San Francisco. The time he and Blanche had visited her sister who lived there on the occasion of the birth of her first child. Three years earlier.

Curly was a much feared gunslinger and he looked a dead ringer for the man who had slugged the sheriff in the afternoon, after he learned the way to Trail's End. Now a man had been gunned down at Trail's End. The curly haired man was missing. Adam Steele was accused of the killing. The Curly Tom Knight knew of was a cold-blooded killer with any weapon. Adam Steele had killed people. But he favoured a Colt Hartford rifle.

So Knight was troubled. Not least by the fact he had not spoken up before the sheriff and the others rode out of town. Troubled enough for the liquor to taste bitter in his mouth. So he left the saloon to go home. Had to pass the livery stable, where he heard talk. Enough to recognise the speakers as Arlene Forrester and Billy Baxter and to realise the woman was planning to go to Trail's End and try to get Steele free, with Billy's help.

Knight, with not enough whiskey inside him to be even slightly drunk, was able to convince Arlene he meant what he said when he offered to help. Not directly with any escape out at the old Sanderson place. But with a room at the boarding house where the Virginian could stay.

Krim had been drawn to the livery when he was about to close up his place and saw the trio talking at the stable doorway. Joined them in time to hear the offer made.

At the time, he now admitted to Steele in the sun-bright attic, he had agreed to be a party to the conspiracy only to the extent of not revealing the unlikely hiding place should he be asked. And when the group eventually returned to Providence with Arlene and Billy as token prisoners of the enraged sheriff, the saloonkeeper kept his promise. Held his tongue as he saw Fallows persuaded not to lock up the black woman and the simpleton in the two cells of the law office—when Lavinia Attwood and Susannah Lineker demanded they, too, should likewise be imprisoned since they had not put themselves out to prevent Arlene and Billy turning Steele loose.

Tom Knight then attempted to tell Len Fallows what he thought he knew about Curly, but the lawman bawled him out for trying to cloud the issue. Steele was guilty as hell in the sheriff's view and his flight was proof of this. And Fallows stormed home, sore headed in more ways than one. While Knight and Harlan Grout got to drinking in the Golden Gate again. And Steele slept himself out of exhaustion up here in the attic.

The saloonkeeper had decided to lend a hand this morning, guessing that in the state he went to bed, Knight was unlikely to be awake until late. Before which time the fugitive would surely need a little sustenance. And maybe some explanations.

Harry Krim had been tending bar a lot of years and, as was customary for one in his line of business, he had listened to countless long and rambling stories of little importance to anyone except the talkers. So maybe this experience was the reason he knew how to relate the basic details of incidents without embroidering them with inconsequentials. Certainly on this occasion Steele was able to finish the mug of reviving coffee without the need to interrupt with questions or to urge the man back toward the point.

The account thus given, Steele poured a second mug of coffee and said: 'I'm real grateful to you, feller. And I don't want to put you to any more trouble.'

'Have to tell you, Mr Steele: I don't want to be put to any more trouble. Especially if it's the kind to get me in bad with local folks. You know how hard it is already for me to make a decent livin' in a town like Providence.'

He looked discomfited again, and Steele thought this was because he was ashamed of the view he had just put forward. But then it emerged the reason was different.

'Somethin' I saved 'til last, Mr Steele.'

'Go ahead, Mr Krim.'

'There's some around here not so rich that a five hundred dollar reward for turnin' you in won't appeal to them, maybe?'

Steele grimaced. 'Who put it up?'

'The Rice woman.'

'I should've guessed. She really put up the money?'

'You mean..? Well, I wouldn't know. Just heard from Harlan it's what she said as the people were leavin' the old . . . your place last night. There'd be five hundred bucks for whoever brought you in. Or give Len Fallows the information that showed him where he could go bring you in.'

Steele now finished the second mug of near cold coffee. Set down the empty mug on the tray alongside the flame-blackened pot. Took off his right glove and extended the hand as he eased to his feet. Said:

'I'm indebted to you, Mr Krim: for the best coffee I reckon I ever drank, and for taking the time to tell me what I'm up against.'

Krim rose, put the crate back where it came from and accepted the handshake. Replied:

'Just doin' what I figure is right, Mr Steele. Ain't cost me no more than a pot of coffee and ain't put me in line to get in trouble with folks hereabouts. I just think, same way Tom does . . . And Arlene and the schoolteacher—even Billy and a few more around here, I guess—that what happened at the old Sander . . . your place . . .

'Well, that ain't your style, Mr Steele. And if it wasn't for Len Fallows havin' his knife in you for what's in the past, since you got here . . . Well, it's my belief there's a whole bunch of other Providence folks think the same way.'

Harry Krim trying to express his feelings was like a different man to the one who gave Steele a report of events in his absence. Only now did he end the handshake. Stooped to pick up the tray. Turned and went to the open doorway. Where he stopped to look morosely back. Watched as Steele put the glove back on then reached to slide the rifle from the saddle boot.

'You know I got no axe to grind, Mr Steele. One way or the other. You ain't a high spendin' customer of mine: nor neither is Len Fallows. Folks hereabouts . . . Well, we're just a bunch of country folks. Ain't none of us perfect, but if nothin' else, we're loyal to our own kind.'

'Sure, Mr Krim,' Steele said as he absently trailed fingertips over the fire-scorched rosewood stock of the Colt Hartford. Touched but did not linger on the inscribed gold plate fixed on the side. 'And there are some who are certain I'll never be one of that kind?'

'But what's right is right,' Krim said, obviously not in direct response to the Virginian's rhetorical thinking aloud. 'Figure most Providence folks know right from wrong. But I got to tell you. Even them that believe you're right and the Rice kind and that Curly guy are wrong . . . Just want you to know, Mr Steele, we ain't about to risk our necks. Won't tell on you. Not for five hundred bucks nor nothin' else. But the rest of it . . . That's your business.'

He went out without waiting for a reply. Closed the door firmly behind him, like this gesture emphasised he truly had done as much as he could to assist the Virginian.

As the footfalls descended the staircase, Krim treading as carefully as when he came up to the attic—like he was afraid his presence in the boarding house might be detected out on the square—Steele flexed his muscles. Then began to move back and forth along the boarded area, the rifle gripped loosely at his side. And soon he felt good enough to experience hunger as the exercise acted with the coffee to stimulate his gastric juices.

He recalled that there were the remains of his trail supplies in a saddlebag and he found two pieces of jerked beef and a chunk of sourdough bread. He ate the meagre breakfast while he stood, walked, sat down and rose. Then he made some fast moves and awkward turns. Before he was ready to acknowledge the worst of his physical discomforts were over: provided he did not take another blow to the small of his back. Where, he was convinced, he must have crashed down on a damaging rock when the curly haired man who could be a San Francisco gunslinger had knocked him off his horse.

Next he made use of a chink in the roof shingles, down

close to the eaves at the front of the house. With hands and knees on two parallel joists and his head bent low and twisted, he was able to get an eye close enough to the small hole to have a fairly wide angle view of the square below.

At first, nothing moved down there except for the building and tree shadows which crawled almost imperceptibly to the dictates of the slow rise of the sun across a cloudless sky. Then a shadow moved more quickly. That of a man carrying something.

Which set Steele's nerves jangling for a second. Until he realised the shadow was thrown by Harry Krim, returning with the tray to the Golden Gate. Long enough after he had left the attic to suggest he had spent some time with Tom Knight.

Other people were up now, Steele saw. But not yet about outside. Chimneys smoked as the storekeepers who lived on their premises across the square cooked up whatever they needed to get their systems going for the day ahead.

Quiet as it was now—or when the town became as thriving as it ever did during business hours—Steele had to allow Providence certainly did look like a good place in which to belong. And now he grimaced as he recalled the final exchanges with Harry Krim. Then he growled softly, cynically—almost self-pityingly—as he began to draw his eye away from the chink:

'Reckon you called it right, Mrs Rice. There really is only one way I'll ever be wanted in any place like this. For a reward.'

9

Voices below to the right drew his attention back to the hole in the roof. But the speakers were beyond his range of vision.

'Mornin', Mr Krim! It sure is a fine one, ain't it? Or it would be, if the boss weren't in so much bad trouble!'

Billy Baxter had started out brightly with the greeting. Then suddenly changed his tone to abject misery as he spoke of the Virginian.

'We all got our troubles, Billy,' the saloonkeeper replied wearily, his voice lower but still loud enough to carry a considerable distance in the early morning quiet. 'But I gotta allow, some have worse kinds than others. You're right, Billy. Troubles apart, it sure is another fine day.'

'I'm takin' real good care of the horses while Mr Steele ain't around to look out for them hisself, Mr Krim.'

'Sure, Billy. He'll be mightly appreciative of you doin' that for him.'

Then Krim started toward the Golden Gate. For like most Providence people he was generally willing to spare a kind word for the mentally retarded man but never had the inclination to get involved in a prolonged conversation.

A third voice intervened: muffled so that the sense of what was said did not reach Steele in the attic. But it was discernible that the man was disgruntled and the Virginian guessed this was probably Harlan Grout. Hungover and complaining at being awakened by the talk.

Then, with the start of a smile on his face, Steele froze as he made to withdraw from the tiny spyhole in the roof. This as he glimpsed on the periphery of his vision a movement of something with more substance than a shadow. In a moment, as the smile became a scowl, the sudden switch from mild amusement to fear acted to churn the coffee and food in his stomach and raise acid bile into his throat.

Len Fallows was striding off Main Street on to the square. Not his usual immaculate self, but unshaved, unwashed and hurriedly dressed in the first clothing that came to hand. Hatless, so the darkly stained patch on his head wound showed. As he moved purposefully along the straight line that was the shortest distance between the end of the street and the front doorway of the boarding house. His left arm swinging while his right hand draped the butt of his holstered revolver.

Billy cried: 'Mr Fallows?'

Even in his retarded mind he could work out from the sheriff's gait and the expression on his bristled, sleep-puffed face, that something was very much amiss.

Harry Krim snarled: 'Aw, shit, no!'

'What the hell?' Harlan Grout demanded to know. Slurred, but now loud enough to be distinctly heard in the attic.

Where Steele backed away and stood up from his secret vantage point. His face impassive as he made to escape from the refuge suddenly become a trap. Sure in his own mind Len Fallows was coming for him.

'Steele!' the lawman roared to confirm it. 'Come on out of there!'

The Virginian stumbled and one foot slipped off a joist to hit the ceiling of the room below: hard enough to punch a hole through it. And in this position he froze again. Just for a part of a second, as the door of the attic was flung open.

Then he moved into series of fluid actions that brought the Colt Hartford into a two-handed grip, the hammer back, the muzzle trained in a rock-steady aim from his hip to the doorway.

Where Susannah Lineker appeared, her slender body trembling and her youthfully pretty face a mask of terror: which altered to threaten a flood of tears as Steele swung away the rifle so that it no longer covered her. She gulped deeply then, a hand going to her throat. Before she rasped hoarsely:

'Adam! I came to warn you! To help you! Come with me, please?'

'You hear me, Steele?' Fallows snarled against a rising background swell of voices: people shocked by the strident interruption to the morning calm of the town in the timber.

'I'm sure getting out of this place!' Steele told the woman, and dragged his foot free of the holed ceiling. But he went to his gear instead of the doorway.

'Hurry, please!'

'Get going. I'll be right behind you.'

'What's goin' on, Len?' It sounded like Harold Archer from the grocery store.

'Sheriff?' This was a woman. Amelia Decker, the wife of the butcher, maybe. Or Faith Kenway who ran the hardware store. Anyone.

'I want you, too, Knight!' Fallows bellowed. 'You're an accessory to the crime of murder and——'

Steele did not make a point of listening now. As he delved into a saddlebag and brought out a carton of shells for the Colt Hartford. Then went to the doorway from which Susannah Lineker had gone. Started after her, hearing her footsteps hurrying lightly down the stairs. Then, too, he heard a voice within the house: a man. His just one of many voices, all the others from outside.

'What's happenin'?' Tom Knight asked sleepily.

'Please, Mr Knight,' Susannah answered fearfully. 'I'm helping Mr Steele.'

Moments later the Virginian went by the open doorway on a landing and saw Knight. Still fully dressed from last night, his bloodshot eyes changing expression from perplexity to dread. He said hurriedly:

'I don't know what could've happened, honest I don't!'

'I know,' Steele told him. 'Real sorry for the trouble, feller.'

Then he ran on down the staircase. Caught up with Susannah in the hallway that cut through the house at ground level. She stopped abruptly and he slowed to keep from slamming into her.

'I have a safe place for you to go, Adam,' she promised earnestly.

'So let's get going,' he snapped curtly. But knew this woman well enough to soften his expression. Before she got tearful because of the harsh way he was treating her. Showed a fleeting smile as he assured: 'I'm grateful for the help, Susannah.'

She responded with a far brighter smile as she swung around and went out the rear door which she had left open. He took the time to close the door then followed her as she frantically beckoned to him. Past the side fence of the livery's corral and into the timber through which he had approached last night, coming then from the north. This morning, hard on the heels of the woman, he went south.

'What're you accusin' me of, Len?' Tom Knight bellowed, his furious demand cutting across the chorus of other voices probably demanding to know much the same thing.

The lawman snarled: 'Get yourself out here, mister! And bring that murdering stranger with you!'

Steele, feeling ungainly as he loped along behind the fleet-footed, slimly built woman, was not able to hear anything else coherently. The widening distance now, as much as the multitude of babbling voices, acting to blur what was being shouted back and forth. Then he was aware of a brief flare of anger at the way Len Fallows had called him a stranger.

Sure, he had said to Harry Krim, then to himself, he would never be entirely one with the people who had lived so much longer than he in and around this country town. But hell, he had been in the Providence River Valley for a year and a half! He was no stranger any more!

Then he and the woman were far enough advanced through the timber to be out of earshot of all that was happening back on the down-town square. And Steele called himself a fool for concerning himself with inconsequentials.

A few moments later, Susannah Lineker suddenly halted and fell to the grassy ground with a kind of corkscrewing motion that reminded Steele of somebody getting shot. On a frontier town street, west of the Pecos trail or an eastern battlefield: this last at a time when the country was in danger of becoming divided north-south rather than east-west.

But the woman was not hurt and Steele once again felt angry for his stupidity in allowing his thoughts to stray along a line that served no useful purpose in the present dangerous circumstances.

Then he needed to control an impulse to irritability with Susannah Lineker. The woman was simply out of breath: or was pretending to be short of breath, he suspected, as he looked down at her and she simpered up at him.

So much of what she did was in the realm of the overly dramatic. In terms, anyway, of how she had endeavoured to attract him over recent months. So he invariably examined everything she did or said from several viewpoints while he reserved his judgment.

Last night at Trail's End, the situation had been too confused for him to take the time to study her emotional outbursts. This morning in the sunlit timber, the knowledge a manhunt would shortly get underway acting to pump sweat from his every pore, he found himself again not disposed to look deeper than the surface of this woman.

Who sat in what seemed to be a carefully posed attitude on the grass. Legs folded beneath her in a way that caused the lightweight fabric of her plain blue dress to hug her slender thighs tightly. Body turned in a manner that accentuated the thrust of her fine, small breasts as she breathed at a quickened rate. While her slightly upturned face expressed a mood not entirely removed from the wantonly seductive.

Hard toned, but holding back from the anger it was tempting to unleash, he told her: 'You're in the lead, lady. But it's not the time nor the place to try to lead me on.'

'But, Adam, I want only to help you! It's what I want so

much to do! But I'm so out of breath after running to the Knight house——'

'So rest awhile,' he cut in. 'If you really do have a place in mind for me, tell me where it is. I'll find my own way.'

'No!' She sprang effortlessly to her feet and reached out a hand to grip his upper arm. Showed the expression of a small girl eager to please he had seen often before. 'No, I'll take you there, Adam. Please let me help you, won't you?'

Now she was breathing no faster than normal, as he tacitly invited her to go ahead. And that was how they moved through the timber for the next few minutes, easily and without speaking. Except for when they had to emerge into the open for a few seconds, to cross the spurs that cut off Main Street and led out to the isolated places east of town. And twice, when they swung around a place too closely and an alert dog, a skittish horse or a cluster of nervous hens gave vent to noisy warnings of their presence.

But a low-toned word of assurance always calmed the woman's anxiety.

Then Steele began to experience a little agitation of his own: this when he suspected they were headed for the place Susannah's parents rent from Josh Marley. This, he knew, would be a bad place for him to hole up.

Firstly since Jake and Ellie Lineker did not share their daughter's affection for him. Secondly, everyone in town knew Susannah had designs on him and so the farm was one of the first places Fallows would look for him.

But then she turned right instead of to the left and he compressed his lips just before he was about to voice his objection.

All around there was pastoral peace except for their footfalls, muffled in the lush grass and leafmould of the forest floor. It was like they were very far removed from any fellow human beings: certainly it did not seem possible they were still so close to town. But then, suddenly, before he realised where they were—he had never come to this part of Providence from this direction before—they were out back of the church in the north east corner of the cemetery.

And Susannah Lineker turned to face him, her back to the fieldstone wall that bounded the well-tended graveyard with its manicured grass and scrubbed stone markers aligned in precise rows. She smiled with pride as she asked:

'Well, Adam, what do you think? It's only Tuesday, you know. And the Marlows are going to be away in Broadwater until Saturday, I've heard. Don't you consider this will be just the perfect place for you to stay? Out of sight and so out of danger?'

He nodded. 'Sure, Susannah. I'm grateful to you for thinking of it.'

'You don't have to be. I'm just happy to be of service.'

'I'll be happier if you don't talk about service,' he said lightly. 'Right here and now.'

She looked at him sharply, anxiously, to ask: 'Adam, are you all right? Do you still feel unwell after what happened to you last night?'

'I'm fine,' he answered the woman who seldom found much in life amusing. Certainly did not share his sense of the ironic. 'It's just the only service that comes to mind around a church right now is the funeral kind.'

She blurted with a grimace: 'Oh, Adam! Please don't!'

He shrugged. 'But this sure is the place for graveyard humour.'

10

This was the first occasion Steele had stepped into the Providence church. But what he saw within the white-painted clapboard walls came as no surprise to him.

Providence was not an excessively religious community but enough of its citizens attended services and lent financial support to ensure that the fabric of the building was well preserved. And the simple furnishings and less than ornate decorations were neatly arranged and scrupulously clean. This, he had heard from Arlene Forrester, was insisted upon by the Reverend Joseph Marlow. And his wishes were lovingly carried out by his wife and a band of devout lady helpers.

At this summer season, wall vases were filled with colourful fresh flowers, their fragrance mingling pleasantly with an underlying scent of wax polish. Which made Steele uncomfortably self-conscious of his unwashed body and dishevelled clothing. He had not washed up nor been out of his clothes since he left night camp many miles to the south some forty-eight hours ago.

Then he was disconcerted for a different reason: as he halted just inside the threshold and looked toward the woman moving up the floor-boarded aisle between the twin rows of pews—heading for the altar. This as his mind was once again host to unbidden notions that had a less than urgent bearing on his current troubles.

For as he watched Susannah Lineker in these surroundings he was vividly reminded of the gossip rife in Providence over the past few months: that getting Adam Steele to walk *down* the aisle with her was what was uppermost in the mind of this woman.

'I think the vestry, Adam?' she said as she halted between the two front pews. Looked over her shoulder and expressed surprise he held back at the open doorway. 'What's wrong? Do you have something against churches?'

He shook his head, reached behind him to close the door. Walked up the aisle, his booted feet ringing hollowly on the boards. Replied: 'Not a thing.'

She wreathed her face with another bright smile and moved off to the side, past the elevated pulpit and went through a curtained archway in back of where a small pump organ stood.

'I know it's tiny, Adam,' she said as he reached the threshold. 'But safety is of paramount importance, don't you think? Over and above comfort, certainly?'

The windowless room was no larger than ten by six. Furnished solely with an old and rickety looking chair. From two pegs to one side of the archway hung clerical garments that were either new or well preserved. Thus the scene fitted in with the character of Joseph Marlow and the way he preferred to serve his congregation. He would wish to look his best in the pulpit, but would feel no need of luxury in this private place where he donned his immaculate surplice and cassock and rested before he conducted services.

'Pardon me?' Steele asked absently as he became aware the woman had said something and was waiting for a response from him.

Her tone mildly rebuking, she said: 'I asked if you agree that it's more important to be safe than comfortable?'

He nodded. 'That's right, Susannah. Especially since I don't reckon to spend too much time in here.'

'You don't?' She was agitated to hear this totally unexpected answer, and looked ready to get angry. 'But why on earth not? I thought you'd need to——'

Steele leaned against the side of the archway as he broke in on her: 'Far as the town sheriff's concerned, he's got me dead to rights, Susannah. Fallows is looking to arrest me and hold me for trial. So it's up to me to prove the Rice woman lied.

Which I can't do by just sitting here in hiding. Thanks, I owe you for what you've done for me.'

'But I——'

'Time's passing, Susannah. Around here it's just the Marlow house that's empty. Pretty soon the rest of the people at this end of the street will be out and about. Best you're not seen leaving the church, I reckon?'

He was conscious of the patronising attitude he was beginning to adopt toward the woman. Which had happened often since he became aware of her romantic interest in him. By so doing he found it a little easier to keep himself from switching from strained politeness to irritable impatience with Susannah Lineker. Either she always elected to suppress resentment toward him for talking to her as if she had the same mental age as Billy Baxter: or she secretly enjoyed it.

Certainly now, as she nodded and chewed on her lower lip, it was easy to think she was purposely working at her little-girl-lost pose again. Then she sighed. 'Yes, you're perfectly right, Adam. Of course you are. People know about us and if I'm gone for too long . . . Well, it's most likely they'll start to put two and two together.'

She looked expectantly at the Virginian, eager to have him agree with her. But he simply inclined his head and stepped out of the curtained archway toward the chair. A move that supplemented his suggestion she should leave. Then, as she went toward the arch, he said:

'Something, Susannah?'

'Yes, Adam?' Excited as she whirled and for a second he thought she was about to launch herself at him and throw her arms around him.

'How did you put two and two together?'

'I'm sorry?'

'Added it up that Len Fallows knew where I was last night. And was coming to arrest me?'

She nodded vigorously, welcoming the opportunity to stay in the church vestry longer. 'By chance, Adam, that's all.

After we got back to town last night—the sheriff and Miss Attwood and the rest of us—I just knew I would never be able to sleep. And that's exactly what did happen. I kept dozing but waking up again. Worried and thinking about where you were and how you were faring. All sorts of thoughts kept coming into my head. You know how you can think some crazy things, sometimes?'

'Yeah, I know,' Steele encouraged her.

'Well, finally, I just got out of my bed, dressed and went for a walk. Foolishly, I hoped I'd come across you, perhaps. But knowing I wouldn't, I guess. Feeling better to be up and about, though. At least doing something that seemed useful instead of just tossing and turning in bed.'

'And?' he pressed, finding it more difficult by the second not to lose patience with the woman.

'It was dawn. First light. Not dark, exactly. But not so easy to see. You know?'

'I know.'

'I was walking along Fir Tree Road, toward Main Street when I saw somebody else was up and about. Don't ask me who. I don't know. Truth to tell, I don't even know if it was a man or a woman. But somebody was just coming away from the Fallows house on Fir Tree Road near the corner with Main, you know?'

'I know, Susannah.'

'Well, there was just something sneaky about the way the person kind of crept away. Then started to run. Not because they'd seen me. Just in a hurry to be gone, soon as they knew the sound of running feet wouldn't wake up the Fallows'.

'Well, it seemed so odd to me, I just had to stay there and watch for a time. I'm not like Faith Kenway—I don't claim it had anything to do with second sight. But I just had a bad feeling. You know how you can get a bad feeling about some things?'

'Sure, Susannah.'

'Well, I did consider going to the sheriff's house. To tell him about the suspicious looking person I saw.'

'But you didn't?'
'No, I didn't, Adam. Len and Molly Fallows were not up right then. The drapes were still pulled and there was no smoke from the chimney. So I just waited and watched. I don't know why. Just that bad feeling. Then the drapes were opened and I heard Molly Fallows call out to Len. Shouting, you understand. Up the stairs. She told him somebody had pushed a note under the door in the night. It said you were hiding at the boarding house.
'Well, the sheriff shouted back down that he'd go straight away to see if what the note said were true. And that's it, Adam. I didn't waste a second. I came running there to the Knight house and, well, you know the rest.'
'Sure, Susannah,' Steele said flatly. 'And you've really no idea who it was left the note?'
'No, Adam. As I said, it could have been a man or a woman. Not big, nor small. Medium size, I guess. With a long coat. And a hat that seemed to be pulled down over their face. I only glimpsed them from the back, though.'
'Thanks again, Susannah.'
'I'm glad I can help you, Adam.'
'Yeah.'
'When should I come back?'
'Uh?'
'Midday, maybe? Or tonight for sure. You'll get hungry, that's certain.'
'I don't reckon I'll starve, Susannah. You've done enough. I don't know how long I'll be here. Or even if I'll come back at all.'
'Not come back?'
'Like I told you, it's up to me to show Lydia Rice is a liar. And I have to start to do that just as soon as the excitement has died down. After people think I've left town. Be easier then to move around. When nobody's looking for me behind every tree. Easier to get back out to Trail's End.'
'Trail's End, Adam? Why?'
'Because that's where . . .' He felt on the brink of losing his

temper. Held on to it by looking away from her face with its plaintive expression. 'It doesn't matter. I'm not sure of my plans right now. Or even if I've got any. I can't be sure when I'll see you again, Susannah. But I will. Like I said, I owe you.'

She continued to stand in the archway for a further few moments, looking hurt at the way he was so eager to have her leave. But at length she said in a pained tone: 'Very well, if you say so, Adam.'

She turned and went out, the curtain falling back into place behind her. In the stillness of the church at this quiet end of town, her footsteps were unobtrusive as she moved down the aisle. She opened and closed the door with no undue noise.

And Steele experienced a stab of guilt as he allowed a sigh of relief to trickle softly from the side of his mouth. Then caught his breath and froze as Susannah Lineker called cheerfully:

'Morning to you, Mrs Daltry!'

'Susannah? Is that you, Susannah Lineker?' Vera Daltry was the near-sighted, eighty-some-years-old widow woman who lived in the first house across the street from the church. This morning she was much closer than her house.

'That's right, Mrs Daltry. My, what lovely flowers. Mother and I often comment on how beautifully you keep the grave of your late husband. How pretty it always looks.'

'That's kind of you to say so, child. And kindly remember me to your mother. And to Mr Lineker, too. It's unusual to see you in the church except at Sunday service?'

Susannah had a reason immediately ready to supply. 'Well, Mrs Daltry, I felt I just had to offer up a prayer for the safe deliverance of Mr Adam Steele. You heard what happened last evening, I suppose?'

'That I did, child. Such goings on in the Providence River Valley. I'm probably speaking out of turn . . . Since I know you like to think of that man as your intended . . . But it does seem to me things have never been the same since he came to live at the old Sanderson place and——'

'I consider you are most certainly speaking out of turn, Mrs Daltry!' Susannah interrupted, her tone almost a snarl. 'Good morning to you. I'll pass on your regards to my parents.'

Steele sat on the hard-seated, straightbacked, unstable chair. Briefly considered the notion Susannah Lineker had purposely started and steered the exchange he had just overheard. Spoke louder than was necessary to the old widow who was almost blind but had excellent hearing.

Then he put the woman out of his mind, not wanting to think too much about the story she had told him: because maybe she had lied as fluently then as when she explained to Mrs Daltry her reason to visit the church on a weekday morning.

But, whatever her motives, she had helped him when Len Fallows came to the Knight house. As Tom Knight had helped him. Harry Krim had done more than Steele would have expected of him. After Arlene Forrester organised his escape. With the eager assistance of Billy Baxter. And it could even be said Lavinia Attwood lent passive assistance by not trying too hard to keep him prisoner at the house—in a battle of wills, Steele was certain the schoolteacher would triumph easily over the black woman.

Now he entered into a battle of his own: for having catalogued those who had helped him in one way or another, he knew it was past time for him to help himself. To get out to where he could prove his innocence. By forcing Lydia Rice to confess or by finding the curly haired man and pressuring him into telling the truth.

This inner conflict was between good sense and reckless impatience. For although he recognised it was necessary to stay in hiding for a while longer—best of all until nightfall—he doubted he could hold out so long. For he thought he might go crazy in this cell-like room which, as time went by, he felt would get to seem more and more like a trap than a sanctuary.

Over a slow-passing hour he became conscious of the steadily rising volume of sound as the south end of Main Street slipped into the quiet rhythm of the new day. Windows and doors opened. People greeted each other. A dog barked. A horse was ridden south at a trot. Then a horse and wagon went north without haste. Finally, footfalls approached the church and the trap image was strengthened.

He heard women's voices, three of them, speaking in tones far removed from the cheerful exchanges of greetings which had been called out earlier. He started to sweat as the women came across the graveyard on the gravel path from the gate. Then, as the church door opened, he realised why these women were here. They were the ones who were to take care of the cleaning chores today.

The door closed and he was able to hear the words rather than just the tones of what was being said.

'—— find that very difficult to credit, Janet.'

'Me, too, Janet. I thought that woman wanted nothing more than to get her hooks into him.'

'Did not we all?'

They stopped, closer to the doorway than the vestry end of the church. And Steele was struck by a thought that squeezed more sweat out of his pores. Then he did a double-take around the walls of the small room, ensured there was no door to a closet in which cleaning materials might be stored. At the same time he saw there was a layer of fine dust on the floor, and cobwebs hung from ceiling corners. So, just as Joe Marlow required no luxuries in the vestry, he was likewise unconcerned with cleanliness in here.

'You'll do the flower vases, Edwina,' Janet instructed. 'And if you'll start on the windows, Lucy dear, I'll dust the pews. Is that all right with us all?'

As far as he was aware, Steele did not know any of these women. Although it was quite possible he would recognise them by sight from having seen them shopping at the town square. Which was unimportant. It mattered only there was a strong likelihood they would recognise him, or guess who he was if they saw him: unwashed, unshaven, in dishevelled clothing, hiding in the vestry with a rifle.

He ran a sleeve over his sweat-sticky face. Consciously worked to keep down the sounds of his breathing as he heard the woman start their chores. One of them began softly to hum a melody that sounded suitably sacred. But she stopped at once when Edwina asked:

'Of course, you know why she did it, don't you?'

'I'm sorry, Edwina dear?' Janet countered.

'The Lineker woman. You know why she left that note at Len Fallows' house?'

Steele made to rise from the chair, but a bone cracked in his lower leg. He swallowed hard at the sound, but soon realised it had not been loud enough to carry outside the vestry.

'A woman scorned, I'd say,' Lucy suggested. 'By all accounts I've heard he's never offered her the slightest encouragement whatsoever. Some say he's hardly ever been civil toward her.'

'I can't really say I blame him for that,' Janet replied. 'A woman who sets her cap at a man the way she did . . . And is spurned by him . . . Well, if she will not take no for the answer, I have every sympathy for this Steele individual.'

'But now she's apparently accepted that he wants nothing to do with her,' Edwina pointed out. 'Realised what a fool she's made of herself. Considers, as Lucy says, she's been scorned. And hell hath no fury . . . I can almost feel sorry for that man.'

'Except that he is a murderer, my dear.'

'Yes, Edwina,' Lucy agreed. 'He had no legal right to move out to Trail's End. So he should have accepted the consequences without resorting to such terrible violence when those with title to the property appeared.'

'Precisely, my dear. I understand this Rice woman who's related to the Sanderson family is foul mouthed and drinks hard liquor. But one must have sympathy with her for being made a widow in such circumstances.'

There was more talk for a while: the women preferring to trade their views on the less than genteel character of Lydia Rice rather than the manner of her widowhood. And Steele listened with mounting impatience, eager for the women to finish their chores and leave. Susannah Lineker had double crossed him. This known, it was now vital to discover her reason. Which was certainly more complex than the woman scorned theory.

The women were silent for a while as they applied themselves exclusively to their cleaning chores. Next became briefly involved in a range of topics from this year's early blooming of flowers to their displeasure that Faith Kenway at the hardware store offered no discount on cleaning materials supplied for use in the church: from the fact that Blanche Knight's sister was getting too old to have another child to how much weight the Reverend Marlow had put on of late.

Then there was a short pause before the women began to chatter again and to make their way from the church: and Steele was struck by the futile notion that the hiatus had probably been for the observance of prayer.

He left the vestry at once, instinctively angling the Colt Hartford across his chest in a double-handed grip, thumb hooked to the hammer, finger curled to the trigger, so that the rifle was ready to be levelled, tracked, cocked and fired in an instant.

The church was presumably now even neater and cleaner than when Susannah Lineker brought him here. But he was in no mood to consider any further useless thoughts. He went to a north side window, close to the angle with the west wall, and peered out through the newly polished glass. Looked across the narrow strip of graveless cemetery, over the top of the wall and along a short stretch of Main Street. To watch as one of the women entered the house next to that of Vera Daltry while the other two went from sight further along the street.

Smoke was curling from a few chimneys but nothing else

seemed to be moving in the sun-bright morning air within the immediate vicinity of the church. Until Steele cracked open the door and pushed his head out. Could see clearly along the empty open trail to the south and up the now deserted street to the north. Now he became aware that birds flew and called. And foliage and woodsmoke was stirred by the lightest of warm summer breezes, that lasted just a few moments.

The timber immediately across from the church could have hidden an army. But it would not be an army of Providence people waiting for Steele to show himself. The trio of devout ladies would not have been allowed to take the risk of entering the church simply as part of a plan to alarm the Virginian into a reckless premature move.

But maybe a gunslinger called Curly—or somebody with curly hair—was lurking over there. Awaiting the opportunity to explode a killing or crippling shot into the man he had helped set the town against.

Aware he was being over cautious, but not feeling foolish because of the care he took, Steele dropped on to his haunches to emerge from the doorway. Stayed below the level of the cemetery wall. Until he was out of sight of the street, in the cover of the side of the church. When he chose speed over cautiousness, took long strides to reach the rear corner of the building.

'Oh, my goodness!' a woman gasped. 'How you startled me!'

Steele had made to swing the Colt Hartford down and around at the exclamation. Then recognised the woman's voice. Froze in the act of bringing the rifle to bear on Vera Daltry. A diminutive lady, no taller than five feet and weighing less than ninety pounds. With a pinched, wrinkled face and greying, thinning hair. Her dress, as always, was the black of mourning to the memory of her many years dead husband.

She stood a few feet back from the corner, in the ten-feet-wide gap between the rear of the church and the cemetery boundary wall. Had obviously just risen from crouching beside one of four graves aligned on this strip of ground. Having placed the last of four single yellow roses into jars sunk into the earth beside wooden, nameless crosses. These graves, Lavinia Attwood had mentioned to Steele, were of four men who had died of yellow fever back when Providence was little more than a cluster of log cabins. Perished without relatives to mourn them, forgotten except by Vera Daltry who each week placed a single flower on each grave.

'I didn't mean to, ma'am,' Steele said as he sloped the rifle to his shoulder and wrenched his mind free of thoughts about dying unmourned.

'I'm sure you did not, sir,' Mrs Daltry excused and brought up a hand to rub her myopic eyes. 'You had no more reason than I to think . . . Oh, my goodness! You're the one who stole the old Sanderson place!'

'Any other time, ma'am,' he said, and moved away from her, 'I'd be happy to talk with you about that.'

He sat on the wall, swung his legs over and dropped down on the other side. The old woman came to the wall, head pushed forward, the better to keep Steele in focus. She said:

'The one the Lineker girl set her sights on!'

Steele was about to growl a sour-toned response that he had better not set his rifle sights on Susannah Lineker. But his attention was suddenly diverted from Mrs Daltry. Toward something that had once been somebody. Until death created a corpse.

'I'm going to have to tell the sheriff I've seen . . . Why, what are you looking at?' Her head came around and she leaned across the wall, to peer intently in the same direction as Steele. 'What on earth is it, man? Why, it looks like——'

'It's Susannah Lineker, Mrs Daltry,' he told her thickly.

'Sus . . . What's wrong with her? Oh, goodness, is she——'

'Someone killed her with a knife, ma'am. And didn't just kill her.'

He started toward the body.

'What do you mean? Didn't just . . .' Quizzically. Then her voice became a shriek. 'It must have been you did it! You're a monster! An inhuman beast! That woman was besotted with you! And you've——'

Steele shook his head in denial as he grimaced down at the blood-sodden, mutilated corpse of Susannah Lineker. And his grip on the rifle tightened to the point of paining his hand as he broke in dully on the shrill, shocked widow.

'I know how she felt about me, ma'am. I wanted to give her the brush off, that's all. I never would have cut her dead.'

11

All the signs pointed to Susannah Lineker having been savagely slaughtered right here where she lay, on the fringe of the timber, some fifteen feet from the cemetery wall. So the first wound would have killed her. Silently, so it and the ghastly mutilation of her body which followed did not alert Steele to what was taking place just a few yards away on the other side of the windowless rear wall of the church.

Almost certainly the slashing open of her throat started the knife attack. As she was grabbed from behind, the killer's hand clamped over her mouth to trap a cry of terror before the blade cut deep. To sever her windpipe and jugular vein, bring almost instantaneous death.

Then the knifer had lowered the warm, limp, blood-spilling corpse to the ground. Spreadeagled her on her back. Sliced the clothing from her torso and limbs. And used the knife time and time again on naked flesh. Slashed or stabbed in a sadistic frenzy. At the thighs, the belly, the breasts and the shoulders.

Because the heart was already stopped for several seconds, relatively little blood had pumped from these wounds. But so many wounds meant the mutilated flesh and the dress and underclothing were saturated in crimson: already crusting to dark brown in the warmth of the summer morning air.

She must have been killed less than a minute after she finished talking with Mrs Daltry and started home over a short-cut through the timber.

While he stood immobile, gazing down at the vicious work of a maniac—or a cold-blooded killer who wanted to make the crime appear like the act of a crazed man—Steele was detached from all else in his surroundings. Unaware of the passage of time. Deaf to every sound. Conscious only of a sense of utter desolation. But abruptly the roaring in his ears was penetrated and ended by a shrill cry that caused him to jerk up his head and wrench it around.

'Murder! He's done it again! That Steele brute has killed the Lineker woman!'

It was Vera Daltry, out front of the church now. Broadcasting at the top of her voice to her fellow citizens her firm conviction about the killing. And as he heard her Steele knew that everyone who learned the grisly circumstances of Susannah's death would share the old widow's belief.

Just for a moment he considered taking the kerchief from around his neck. Using the length of silken fabric with two weighted corners to cover the face of the woman. To veil her death mask which was an expression of abject terror: the skin stretched taut, the wide eyes glazed and the gaping mouth filled with blood. But those who knew him well would recognise the thuggee scarf as belonging to him. And it was certain Fallows would regard it as physical evidence of his guilt and a sign of his remorse.

Other voices were raised. Further along the street. But he had no inclination to stay and listen to what was being yelled back and forth. So, once more, he plunged into the trees to use them and the undergrowth on the forest floor as cover for an escape. Knowing his situation was more perilous than ever.

Before, the townspeople had been divided, albeit unequally, in their opinions about his guilt or innocence in the shotgunning to death of Elmer Rice. Soon they would be united.

Elmer Rice was a stranger, an outsider who, along with his foul-mouthed, liquor-drinking wife, had made an unsavoury first impression on the insular and largely straitlaced citizens of Providence. And some people knew Steele well enough to make allowances for him. A few maybe would even secretly condone the killing of Rice in a rage: if the Virginian truly believed the newcomers were in the wrong.

But Susannah Lineker: she was one of their own. Born of parents who were among the earliest settlers in the Providence River Valley. The woman herself had lived here all her life. The way the killing had been staged, the degree of viciousness used pointing to the unleashing of a terrible spiteful rage, seemed to lay it firmly at the door of Adam Steele: so well did the murder fit into the known facts about the victim and the man everyone knew she had loved and lost.

Steele moved with caution again through the trees which shaded without cooling him. Listening for sounds of pursuit, and endeavouring to avoid undue noise which could draw the pursuers to his trail. For people would be on his trail at once, he knew. Without waiting for word to be sent for Fallows to form and deputise a lawful posse. This killing of a local woman was sure to inflame the passions of people who had known her all her life. And once they caught up with the man they were certain had inflicted such a frenzied attack on the defenceless woman who had been so struck on him...

He had reached the edge of the timber on the east side of a bend in Main Street. There were no houses and no spurs cutting off along this stretch and he was about to cross. For he had the glimmer of an idea that meant he needed to get to the other side of the street. But then he had to halt the move, breathless and sweating. Backed off from the fringe of the trees, crouched down beside a thicket, as footfalls beat on the hard-packed surface of the trail-like street. People running from the south. From where the slashed and bloodied corpse of Susannah Lineker lay.

Two youngish women, one carrying a baby and the other holding the hand of a girl of thirteen or so, came running into sight, panting with exertion or shock. And went on around the curve in the street. Out of his sight, they began to yell.

'Murder! Steele's killed again!'

'The Lineker woman!'

'Stabbed her to death at the church!'

'He has to be found!'

Steele was unsure of exactly where he was in relation to the spurs off Main Street. Now discovered he was close to a house. For voices, a man's and a woman's, began to call shocked responses to the news of another killing.

He rose, advanced slowly to the side of the street, glanced quickly in both directions, then broke out across the open width, plunged into the trees on the other side. Recalled how he and Susannah had crossed several spurs in this way between the Knight house and the church. Then thought only of his pursuers: hotter on his trail than Fallows would have been earlier this morning. And hot with anger, too. Maybe even ready to lynch him should they get him before the lawman came on the scene.

A bunch of ordinary, decent, country town people who had resented him from the start. Knowing much of his past. And how he had dealt with trouble since he came to Trail's End. People willing to kill, as a righteous group, in the way they considered he killed as a vengeful individual. For vengeance, with viciousness. Uncaring at the heated moment for how they would live with the memory of their act in the future.

As he had killed Susannah Lineker. A woman who had loved him. But who he had spurned. A woman who had sought to take revenge of her own: by betraying him to the law. A woman who had died so awesomely by his hand when he discovered the truth of what she had done.

But almost that whole version of events was wrong!

Sure, Susannah had delivered the note to Fallows: never counting on being seen. But only as part of a half-baked ploy to win his gratitude, which might develop into something else. Gratitude for her coming to the Knight house, to warn him and take him to a new safe hiding place. A crazy and highly dangerous plan. But women in love—the kind of a woman this was, anyway—cared nothing for danger. And acted crazy.

But somebody had witnessed the escape from the rooming

house. Followed them to the church. Waited for the chance, and supplied a tragic twist to the woman's plan. Killed her in a way that would make everyone sure Adam Steele was responsible.

The birds throughout the entire timbered valley in which the town was situated now seemed to be silent. Maybe they had been so ever since Vera Daltry had started to shriek the news of the killing?

Behind him, far off, voices were raised: too distant for the words to carry to him, even for the tone to be discerned. But he could guess the people's feelings.

Then he came upon his first objective. Emerged at the rear of the place where Arlene Forrester lived. At the end of a narrow track which angled off Mission Farm Road, finished at the black woman's riverside cabin. Which was a one-roomed, timber building half the size of the house at Trail's End. Set on the centre of an area of hard-packed dirt bounded by trees on three sides and the slow-flowing Providence River on the other. At this point the river's hundred-feet width was in sight for a quarter mile curve, it's surface dazzlingly bright in the brilliant sunlight of a day now advanced past mid-morning.

Smoke rose lazily from the stove stack that angled out of a side wall of the cabin and a smell of steam emanated from the place. The mare Arlene rode out to Trail's End and to other isolated places where she did paid chores stood on a patch of cropped grass in the shade of an oak. Just her tail moved, to flick at bothersome flies. Then the Negress's voice intruded morosely on the stillness that was now hardly disturbed by the hue and cry which seemed to have lessened in impetus. She started to sing a mournful spiritual about strife, sin, death and Judgment Day.

The far bank of the river was thick with timber: the nearest place out that way was Abe and Rose Steiners' Mission Farm, something over a mile away. So Steele was able to hunker down on the river's edge on this side, drink from his cupped palms and splash water on his sweat-run face with no risk of being seen.

And it was suddenly tempting to rest there for a while: indulge the ache in his back which now troubled him for the first time in a long time. Even to strip off his clothes, take a bath in the cool, cleansing river. Wait for the pursuit to totally fade. But, if he needed truly to rest up, this was not a good place to do so. For as soon as people realised they had lost his trail—if they had, in fact, ever got on to it—they were sure to start to look for him first in the more obvious places where their quarry was likely to go to ground. And Arlene Forrester's cabin was certainly in this category.

So, feeling as refreshed as he was likely to be for quite a while, he moved out of the trees into the open yard. As yet undecided whether to steal the mare or to request the loan of the horse. If he stole it, he would have to ride bareback, for the saddle was nowhere to be seen—probably in the cabin. But this was not a prime consideration as he went around the corner from the rear to the side of the cabin, neither of which had windows in the clapboard walls under the flat tin roof.

He was indebted to Arlene and maybe something of what he owed her was an explanation of his intentions. But such an account would make her even more of an accessory than she already was. And to a second murder, the nature of which would deny her any of the kind of sympathy that had kept her out of a law office cell last night. So, on balance . . .

But the decision was made for him as he reached for the mare's reins which were hitched to a low-hanging bough of the oak. The sound of Arlene's singing abruptly rose in volume. This as she stepped out of the cabin's only door, which was at the front. And then she cut short the dirge-like spiritual as she sensed she was not alone. Gave a choked cry of alarm as she turned and saw Steele. Almost dropped the basket of sodden laundry she had been about to hang on a drying line where several freshly washed garments were already pegged.

'Mr Steele, sir . .?'

She had recovered quickly, relieved to recognise the intruder, know he meant her no harm. Something close to a smile touched her round and shiny face, beaded with sweat from the steamy, overheated atmosphere within the cabin. But then she frowned, like she had acknowledged to herself the first expression was inappropriate to the circumstances. Showed concern matched by her tone as she completed: 'Lord, Mr Steele. Whatever is you doin' here? You look in such bad shape, sir, and I——'

He interrupted: 'I need to steal your horse, Arlene.'

'Lord, Mr Steele. You don't have to steal nothin' from me. Nothin's pretty close to what I've got, but anythin' I do got you can have and willin'.'

'I know, Arlene. But something's happened. Something it's best you find out about for yourself later.'

She seemed on the point of pressing for her curiosity to be satisfied. But suddenly stooped her bulky body to put the basket of wet laundry on the ground. Said as she turned and started back into the cabin: 'I'll get the saddle for you, Mr Steele sir.'

She was inside for a few seconds, and when she re-emerged there was a babble of distant voices being carried through the timber again. Along with rustling of foliage. By a new summer breeze. And Arlene paused, head cocked, listening intently. Had no need to advance further, for Steele led the docile mare toward her.

'I heard somebody told on you to the sheriff this mornin',' she said as he took the saddle from her, showed her a fleeting smile.

'I'm grateful, Arlene.'

She peered hard at him, a deeper frown on her face, which mostly in normal times beamed her happiness with her far from easy lot. Said with feeling: 'You surely do look in a bad way, Mr Steele. It has somethin' to do with all that ruckus I can hear?'

'Why don't you go find out, Arlene?' he suggested as he placed the saddle on the back of the mare. Made to boot the rifle before he recalled this was not his saddle.

'I sure hope,' she began as he crouched to fasten the cinch, that it ain't on account of me tellin' that Lineker woman where she could go see you, Mr Steele sir? But she was so pitiful when she come here last night——'

'The noise is on account of me,' Steele broke in, crushing an impulse to anger. 'Something I'm wrongly accused of doing. Since I'm taking your horse and saddle, it's best nobody knows you were here while I did the taking. Natural for you to go find out what all the fuss is about. You won't have to tell any lies about pretending you didn't know already. And it's better they think I stole your property while you were away from the house.'

He swung up astride the saddle and looked down into her puzzled face. Read in her eyes the questions that were forming in her mind. Then saw she came to the decision he wanted her to make.

'Whatever you say, Mr Steele. You take care of yourself, you hear. And you do what you gotta so we can all get back to normal out at Trail's End—you and Billy and me.'

'What I intend, Arlene. How's Billy doing?'

'He's still at Harlan Grout's livery stable, takin' care of your horses, Mr Steele. Far as I know. You want somethin' to eat? You can steal some food, uh?'

'No thanks, Arlene.'

'Good luck to you, Mr Steele sir.'

'Grateful to you, Arlene. I'm about due some luck that isn't the bad kind, I reckon. You want to go and find out what the shindig is about now?'

The distant sound of voices had faded again, for the women spreading the news had moved further north. Toward the square where maybe Len Fallows was back in his office, after failing to pick up the trail of Steele and Susannah from the Knight house.

'Yes, sir, I'll do that,' the black woman agreed. And hurried away, out of the unfenced yard and on to the track that led to Mission Farm Road. Still wearing her wash apron, leaving the basket of sodden laundry abandoned on the ground. A scene that fitted with her being curious and worried about the distant disturbance.

Steele watched her until she was out of sight around a curve in the narrow track. Briefly wondered if she could carry off the sham of total ignorance about his latest escape. Then experienced concern that even if she managed this, Len Fallows—coming to the decision himself or pressured into it by the incensed townspeople—might nonetheless lock her in a cell. Because it was her freeing of the Virginian from the house at Trail's End that gave him the opportunity to kill Susannah Lineker. And then it occurred to Steele that Tom Knight might already be imprisoned in the law office. Put behind bars by the sheriff out of sheer frustration: the need to do something after the morning incident which came in the wake of that of the previous night.

Then Steele grimaced sourly, canted the rifle to his shoulder and urged the reluctant but obedient mare into the river. Told himself he had no time right now to be anxious on account of other people. Impassioned as they were over the gruesome killing out back of the church, the citizens of Providence would not do harm to those who had helped Steele after the shooting at Trail's End. Have them locked up, maybe. With the intention of eventually seeing them legally tried for what they did. But their spite would stop at that, for nobody could have foreseen what Susannah was going to do: and what Steele would do to repay her for the betrayal.

Once in the river, the mare relished the coolness of the water. Until she was out of her depth, when she made to panic and wheel back for the east bank. Gently but firmly, Steele kept her headed in the opposite direction. And, obviously for the first time in her life, the horse instinctively stayed afloat by paddling her legs. Then she was afraid again, but confined her response to a snort, when her forehooves sank into the yielding river bed.

A few seconds later, horse and rider were up on the west bank, in the thick timber, both shedding water. And Steele listened to the stillness that seemed more solid than before, after the splashing and snorting of the river crossing. But birds were calling, and foliage rustled in the breeze that continued to waft gently across the valley. No voices reached from town to this side of the Providence River, which made appealing trickling sounds as it flowed smoothly southward: from its distant source at the lake that gave the town of Broadwater its name, to the much further away Pacific Ocean.

Not so long ago, the Virginian caught up in the kind of dangerous circumstances that centred upon him now might well have contemplated putting a great distance between himself and the trouble. But not now!

He swung out of the saddle and began to lead the mare by the bridle through the thickest of the timber and tangled area of undergrowth. Then could not avoid the notion that, although he might have considered running in the old days, he would never have done so. The killings were too closely tied to him. And in no circumstances would he be able to find peace of mind knowing he had been manipulated into taking the blame for them.

In the old days, too, he would never have spared the time to feel concern for those who chose of their own volition to help him, even at risk to themselves: for back then he cared only for himself. But such days were gone and life was more complex now: as he endeavoured to fit into this community where there never had been much encouragement in many quarters. But hell, it had been his choice to give it his best shot. Irrespective of anything the less than friendly townspeople and his ruling fates did to dissuade him.

He directed a globule of saliva forcefully at the ground, like he was spitting out all memories of the past.

Away from the river, the trees thinned, the ground between them richly carpeted with grass nurtured on leafmould. And as he swung back into the saddle, uncomfortably conscious of the soggy dampness of his booted feet and lower legs, he ran a hand down the neck of the animal, murmured pensively:

'Reckon there are better ways to cross a river. But if there ever was a bridge there, it wasn't one of them I've burned.'

12

It took him a long time to get to Trail's End.

He made a wide swing to the west, to pass at a distance Mission Farm and the other outlying places scattered along this side of the valley. Stayed far enough up on the wooded valley side never to gain sight of the houses and barns he knew were there. Once did pass a fence, in need of repair, that bounded the western extreme of Gerry Chisholm's ranch. Occasionally heard the lowing of cattle or the whinny of a horse.

The mount he had chosen to get, from one of the few people in town he could still trust not to betray him, was past her prime. Out of condition, too, from being ridden so infrequently and so sedately by Arlene. In part it was out of his feelings for the old mare that he travelled at such an easy pace. But, in the back of his mind, was the notion that should events call for a sudden spurt of speed, best the animal have as much wind as possible.

On his own account, he made the journey slowly because he could see no reason, other than impatience, for haste. Trail's End might occur to Fallows, or somebody else, as a place where Steele was likely to run. And the casually paced ride along a route that more than tripled the distance from Arlene Forrester's cabin to the ranch allowed time for people to check the place if they so chose.

But it was equally possible, of course, that the spread would be regarded as his last resort. And certainly the taking of the horse was designed in part to sow the seeds in people's minds that he had fled much further away. Which conviction would serve another purpose if lodged in the mind of Lydia

Rice: of lulling her into a false sense of security, putting her off her guard. Her and the curly haired man should he be holed up at Trail's End.

For the greater part of the way, Steele was on unfamiliar ground, saw landmark features of the valley from fresh viewpoints. One such was High Point Hill with the distinctive stand of timber on its crest. This rise was at the extreme north west corner of the three and a half thousand acres of the Trail's End spread. And once he saw it he then found it difficult to hold to the walking pace. To curb the impulse to demand a gallop toward the property he could not contemplate belonging to anyone but himself.

But from where he first glimpsed the hill there remained a considerable distance to cover and he still had no idea what brand of trouble awaited him at Trail's End. So he maintained the walk as he angled his mount to a new course. Heading south of High Point Hill, to reach the wire-strung western boundary fence at about the midway point between the north and south extents of the spread. Briefly he considered breaking through the fence to approach the house from this direction: but the prospect of forcing a way on to his own property rankled and he immediately put the idea out of his mind.

He rode to the south end of the fence, then turned east. At no time was he able to see the house and barn, for hilly and timbered terrain intervened. Finally, when the day was well advanced into afternoon, he emerged from the trees on to the spur alongside Timber Creek, a few yards short of the gate that still hung open.

Because of the hard-packed surface of the trail and the constant use it was put to, it would have required close study to spot fresh signs which might or might not have told him something of importance. Better, he decided, to find out at first hand the situation on the spread, rather than to try to make educated guesses about it.

So, relying just a little on his no longer finely honed sense for being observed by hostile eyes, he went through the gateway on to the place. At once felt more composed than at any time since he turned away from the butchered body of Susannah Lineker. Calm, but not complacent, as he shifted the rifle from where it rested across the saddlehorn to cant it to his right shoulder. Thumb to the hammer and finger curled on the trigger.

Knew as accurately as if he had been looking into a mirror the kind of impassive expression that had formed on his heavily bristled, sweat-beaded face. Impassive, but with latent brutality just beneath the surface. This hinted at by the degree of hardness in his coal-black eyes, and the suggestion that the almost closed lips were a split second away from drawing back to reveal the teeth in an animalistic snarl.

It was the kind of expression that used to take control of his face time and time again. But not so often since he settled at Trail's End. The kind of expression which, if the good people of Providence saw it, would convince them—if they were in any doubt—that this man was entirely capable of doing what had been done to Susannah Lineker.

He rode to within sight of the house, reined in the docile mare at the point where the track started between the crop fields. Alongside the thicket out of which the man with curly hair had lunged to knock him off another horse last night.

He sat virtually immobile: raked his eyes one way and then another along their narrowed sockets. Saw with what seemed an incredible degree of clarity every visible feature of the house, the barn, the corral, the yard, the crop fields, a length of Timber Creek and the rolling acreage beyond these features at the foreground of the sunlit scene. Like he was looking at everything through a gigantic magnifying lens which enabled him to examine each individual blade of grass, hump in the ground, stone of the house walls, knot hole in the timber side of the barn, nail head holding the corral fence together.

He chose not to look closely at any single feature of the scene. But he did, over perhaps ten seconds, see and sense enough to be certain the place was deserted.

It was ominously quiet, too. Birds called and foliage rustled in the breeze. Timber Creek trickled. But these sounds came from outside the central focus of his concern. Where, even if there was no human presence save his own, chickens should cluck, a hog grunt, maybe, or a milk cow low.

But although there was an eerie quality to the stillness, Steele did not relate it to danger.

He was about to heel the mare forward when something caught and held his attention. Seen out of the corner of his left eye. And he felt even more self-possessed, more confident of resolving this trouble, when he recognised the hat dislodged when he was sent crashing to the ground last night.

He dismounted, retrieved the Stetson from where it lay in the wheat field and thudded it against a leg to shake it free of dust before he set it on his head. Led the horse by the bridle along the five hundred feet of track and on to the yard. Where the pervading silence against a background of the unobtrusive sounds of nature seemed more intimidating.

He went to the barn, swung open one of the double doors and detected the unpleasant smell of dried blood trapped within the building. The mare whinnied her unease at the same stink.

They had slaughtered the milk cow, and the hog. And the hens. The laying chickens and pig were strung up from a roof rafter. The much heavier cow lay on her side nearby, a section of hindquarter inexpertly hacked out of the freshly killed, unskinned animal. But somebody had preferred chicken to beef: a head, the claws and a heap of feathers were all that remained of one bird.

The carcases were stored in the barn area of the building. And the mare became less uneasy when Steele, the brutal streak of his character rising nearer to breaking through the surface of his expression, led her along to the stable end. Unsaddled her, gave her hay and oats and ladled some water from a storage barrel into the trough in the stall.

Did all this with studied deliberation, using the chore of tending to the needs of a horse as a kind of therapy. Which kept him from unleashing his fury in a series of violent and futile actions that would serve no purpose other than to ease the rage he felt at the wanton, clumsily inexpert slaughter of the domestic stock. If such emotion did demand release, he was clear-headed enough to reason, better to wait until those responsible for the senselessly wasteful killing came within range of his anger.

The horse taken care of, he emerged from the barn which had become a slaughterhouse, closed the doors firmly behind him. He was about to go to the front of the house but, as with the hat earlier, glimpsed on the periphery of his vision something that was out of place.

A mound of freshly dug earth in the gap between the front of the barn and the kitchen end of the house, a few feet back from the bank of Timber Creek. It looked like an unmarked grave and he guessed it was where the body of Elmer Rice was buried. The shovel used for the digging lay on the ground nearby.

Having moved close to the elongated mound it was quicker to enter the house through the rear door. But whichever entrance he used, the throat-constricting first impression would have been much the same. Which should not have come as too much of a shock, he thought briefly. Since he knew the people who had moved into the place were the kind capable of wanton killing, be the victims beast or human. So he should not have been even mildly surprised they had systematically wrecked the interior of the one-room house. Not just used his home to eat and get drunk and sleep in. This they had done.

And he had expected it: would maybe have felt little worse toward them on account of the chicken bones and beef gristle spat on the floor, the uncleaned cooking pots and plates, litter of empty and smashed bottles and glasses, and the vomit.

But, elated from the achievement of taking over Trail's

End and having Steele accused of murder, they had carried their celebration beyond excesses of food and drink.

Books had been spilled from the shelf and many were ripped apart. Framed paintings were down off the walls, torn to shreds. The contents of a chest and a clothes closet were strewn across the floor. Two of the four chairs from around the pine table had been smashed, splintered parts of them apparently used to fuel the stove fire on which the chicken and beef were cooked. Stains, maybe just of hurled aside food and liquor, marred the whitewashed walls.

Everything, it seemed, which had contributed to making the once derelict shell of a shack into the home it had become was smashed, torn, mutilated or defiled.

With a furious vengeance. As if those responsible were driven by a burning hatred for the man who had worked so long and hard to transform the abandoned house and spread into a fine place on which to live and make a living.

Hate him, and resent what he had done: which, he began to reflect, did not fit with the idea of the rightful claimant coming to the old Sanderson place for her inheritance. Whether to live there or to sell the property. In either instance, such a rightful heir, although naturally angry at the man who had squatted here, would surely make use of what he had achieved? Not destroyed it out of spite? Or in a desire to raise hell?

Maybe, he reflected as he righted an overturned chair and sat at the table, used the barrel of the Colt Hartford to sweep the mess of greasy plates and cutlery to the floor, a volatile mixture of guilt and fear had something to do with the orgy of gluttony and destruction? As Lydia Rice and her curly haired partner in evil contemplated the escape of Adam Steele. Knew they had no more right to be here than he did. Worried about him returning.

As he had returned now.

He did a double-take. First there had been the hat in the wheatfield. Then the new grave between the house and barn. Now a dark stain on the floor: in the corner between the cold stove and the shattered window.

Just part of the stain was visible, soaked into the hard-packed dirt. The same colour as the blood which had oozed from the shotgun-blasted corpse of Elmer Rice. This mark of last night's violence was totally out in the open. Whereas the second one was partially obscured by a blanket, which had been brought from the bed at the far end of the room seemingly for the express purpose of covering the stain.

Forcing his mind to remain clear, uncluttered by disturbing notions that had no foundation in fact, Steele rose from the chair. Went around the table to the corner of the room. Used the muzzle of the Colt Hartford to raise the blanket and move it aside. Revealed the large stain in its entirety. Raised the blanket high and craned his neck so he could see there was also an area of blood staining on the fabric.

He slanted the rifle so the blanket slid off the barrel, and looked down again at the darkened area on the dirt: which suggested so much blood had been lost that somebody other than Elmer Rice must surely have died in this house. Some time after Rice was blasted to death last night. How long ago, he was not prepared to guess. But today, he felt sure.

He left the house. By way of the rear doorway again, because that was the quickest way to the grave. Rested the rifle against the fieldstone chimney which ran up the outside wall of the house and took up the shovel. Gingerly, he began to shift dirt, off the mound, then out of the hole: unwilling to visualise what—who—was buried there. Allowing his emotions to react without preconceived ideas to whatever new aspects of this blood-soaked business would be revealed in a few minutes.

He soon discovered he had been right to work carefully with the shovel. Having assumed the kind of people who killed as these did would not take too much trouble with the digging of a grave. It would be a shallow one. And so when it became necessary to bury a second body—in the same grave to conceal the fact of another killing—there would not be much depth available.

Little more than six inches below ground level, the blade

of the shovel came up against a solid object. And Steele dropped to his haunches, used his gloved hands to scrape away the dusty dirt. To uncover a booted foot that told him nothing. He removed some more dirt and found the matching boot of the pair.

Sank the shovel into the soil beneath these partially exposed feet and knew by the easy way the blade went into the ground for eighteen inches before it was stopped that he had been right. Elmer Rice was buried just a little deeper than the corpse he had started to uncover.

He realised he was filling time with a line of thought that was immaterial: as an exercise in forestalling the inevitable. Because he felt sick to his stomach. Not to be in the presence of death: hell, in retrospect it was easy to think of his life as comprised of little else but one corpse after another: not a few of them dead because of him.

With the threat of nausea came a sudden weakness, that got worse as he struggled to force the acid bile back down his throat. The shovel in his hands felt impossibly heavy, and he found he could not face the prospect of using it to lift more dirt out of the grave.

Nor could he trust himself to do the work delicately. Was afraid he would rush at it, thud in the blade of the shovel and hurl the dirt frantically away: maybe stab the blade into the body and sever some part of it. Unfeeling though the flesh would be, this prospect heightened the danger of retching.

He dropped to his haunches, took hold of a booted foot in each gloved hand. Half rose, backed away. Watched with unblinking eyes, wide enough to cause pain in his eyelids, as the legs, the belly, the chest, the shoulders, then the head between the limply trailing arms came into view.

Dirt still clinging to the clothing. Clothing he recognised. So he had no need to see the familiar face. Nobody around Providence wore quite the same kind of dungarees as Billy Baxter.

Or maybe a whole bunch of men did. Many of them of much the same height and build as the mentally deficient man with the acne-scarred, bug-eyed face who Steele looked down upon. After gently resting the feet on the ground and unfolding upright.

But nobody else, wearing blue denim dungarees or any other kind of garb would feel the need to come out to Trail's End. To see to it the stock of his boss was being cared for. The hog and the chickens fed, the cow milked.

Which was surely why Billy had forsaken the chore of guarding the horses in the livery. Maybe after Harlan Grout got irritated with having Billy around. Sent him out of the stable with a promise to take care of the horses, which was his job he was getting paid to do.

And Billy, not understanding entirely what had happened and was happening, but knowing Steele was in no position to look out for the stock at Trail's End, had come here to...

Steele shook his head. Made the physical move to dislodge such a thought process from his mind. For the details were irrelevant right now. It mattered only that Billy Baxter had come here. And for some reason had done something, innocently to his retarded mind, that had caused someone to slash open his throat. In just the way as the throat of Susannah Lineker had been brutally cut.

Here, the knife had not then been used to mutilate the body afterwards. For there had been no purpose to be served by so doing. Immediately, or pretty soon after the killing, the new grave was re-opened and the body was buried. And the stain made by the torrent of blood from the gaping wound had been carelessly covered.

Again, Steele realised with a choked grunt, he was entering into the realm of supposition, which was pointless: Billy was dead. And although there was no sign to point to the fact that this killing was going to be blamed on him, the Virginian felt more incensed by it than the murder of the woman. It was inevitable he would be, of course.

He moved to the side of the corpse. Dropped to his knees, pushed his arms beneath Billy's shoulders and thighs and came to his feet. No longer felt sick or weak as he carried the dusty burden into the house, the head and an arm hanging limply at one side and the legs at the other. Took care as he stepped in through the rear doorway that the unfeeling flesh of the dead man did not bang into the frame at either side.

He carried the lightweight body to the far end of the wrecked room and lowered it gently on to the dishevelled bed. Straightened and ran a sleeve over his face. Needed to fist salt moisture out of his eyes, knowing without shame the stinging sensation in them was not caused entirely by sweat erupted by the heat or the day and the recent exertion.

Told Billy in a thick-toned voice: 'Be a while yet before I can allow you to rest in peace, feller. But when the time comes, it'll be done right. No expense spared. Cost in money or lives.'

13

It was the opposite of his slow ride from town to Trail's End. For now he had no idea of how much time there was to do what was needed: so he worked fast. But he was thorough, as he prepared for the return of Lydia Rice and her curly haired partner.

He had started to think of them always as a pair now, without knowing their connection. For they were certainly partners in causing so much to go badly wrong with his life over the past twenty-four hours. That was for sure.

While he worked he listened for the first sounds to signal the return to Trail's End of these two people he intended to kill. And, when he was in a position to do so, he also kept watch out along the track between the crop fields to the point where anyone approaching the house would first come into sight.

Only once did he consider the possibility they would not come back.

Having tired of the confidence trick they had played on the people of Providence.

Or grown bored with the wanton killing in this neck of the woods.

Perhaps, even, frightened off by the unexpected need to kill the poor, benighted Billy: a crime they knew they would not be able to blame on Adam Steele.

For whatever reason, taken off for pastures new. In the knowledge that they had no legal claim to the spread.

Considered them leaving, but quickly rejected it after reflecting upon these possible motives for their departure. Because, even if they started to ride the hell away from the

Providence River Valley, the Virginian felt himself capable of influencing them to turn right around and come on back: by the sheer power of willing them to do as he required. And what he required was to get within killing range of the couple: so badly, he was confident anything was possible to achieve this end. Even the supernatural, if the superhuman was unattainable.

Which was crazy, but he had sure felt crazy since he dragged on the buried boots and discovered Billy Baxter was wearing them.

The afternoon had almost run its course when he was through. Evening was beginning to descend over the rolling country of the Sierra Nevadas western foothills. And it was that twilight time when nothing appears real: solid objects can seem mere shadows and there are shadows of solid objects that do not exist.

From where he waited and watched, dry-eyed and free of sticky sweat now, washed up and shaved, one hand loosely fisted around the frame of the Colt Hartford, he had a clear view of the yard and its immediate surroundings. And, without relaxing his vigilance, he allowed unrelated memories to come and go at random through his mind: not consciously considering this as helping him to stay on the sane side of a narrow line.

Visualised the buildings and the corral when he had first seen them, derelict and falling down.

Clay Murchison nailed to a chair in the yard.

The terrified Billy Baxter about to be hacked to pieces with an axe by a hired hand who was a good man at the best of times, a crazed killer at the worst.

Being awakened in the house in the dead of night by an old-timer and a homicidal kid wielding a baseball bat.

Billy again, beaten senseless, tied to the corral fence.

But not all the memories were bad.

Arlene Forrester, singing a joyful gospel song as she cooked a meal on the stove, the mouth-watering aroma of the food wafting out across the yard. Into the barn or the corral where Steele was working.

Lying in bed at the end of a long, hard, satisfying day. Reading one of the books he had purchased as part of a batch of household chattels from a pair of disenchanted settlers who were about to move back east.

Alone in the bed: just infrequently acknowledging his new-found home would never be complete until he shared it—and the bed—with a wife.

But not the over-dramatic, quick-to-tears, less than bright, little-girl-lost in middle age Susannah Lineker. Who had tried so pathetically hard to interest him. Too hard, without the wits to recognise that just as she was not Steele's type of woman, so he was not her kind of man. Or maybe this hapless woman who never meant harm to anyone had simply gotten desperate. Would have set her cap at any new unattached male who came to town. Having exhausted her opportunities with all the bachelors and eligible widowers already settled in the Providence River Valley.

Hooves hit the hard-packed dirt of the spur that came up from the main Providence to Broadwater trail. More than two horses, ridden at a trot through the gateway and on to the track that continued to follow Timber Creek all the way to Trail's End.

He had expected to hear just two horses. Or maybe even one. But experienced no impulse to anger. Nor disappointment, frustration, certainly not panic. Watched and waited. Then was briefly irritated with himself that the sound of the hooves brought to mind an image from far back in his past. Of a column of cavalry. Grey-clad men, himself a lieutenant at the head of the double file of CSA troopers.

But this was no troop of uniformed men. Certainly not in grey so long after the end of the War Between the States. Nor in blue: called upon by the town as once, not so long ago, Len Fallows had set out to call in the United States Army to deal with local trouble that had gotten too much for him to handle.

This was a bunch of civilians, almost all of them

Providence citizens. Dressed in business suits, work coveralls, aprons and Sunday best dresses: for there were women as well as men. Clearly seen in the bright, glittery light of the moon shining from a cloudless sky.

At the head, a man and a woman who Steele, in other circumstances, may have needed to look at twice to recognise. Now, because of recent events, he knew them immediately. The skinny, unbeautiful Ellie Lineker. And her beefily built, nearly bald, thickly black bearded husband, Jake.

Behind these rode Arlene Forrester and Tom Knight. Not here of their own free will: their hands, bound at the wrists, tied to the horns of their saddles. The mounts they sat were led on lines by men who rode at either side to form a four-abreast line. These were two of the town storekeepers: Harold Archer and Ronald Decker.

Then came two people Steele had seen only briefly at other times of actual or impending violence: Lydia Rice and the curly haired man. Flanked by the newspaperman, Huey Attrill, and Michael Morrison, for once without his mother nearby.

Following were a dozen men and women the Virginian knew, either by name or, mostly, by sight.

Noticeable by their absence from the column that now came to a clustered halt on the yard were Len Fallows and Lavinia Attwood.

Since there was a score of people and their mounts on the yard, there could not be silence in the night. But when the column had come to a halt, the pause following the clattering of so many hooves seemed only a degree removed from utter soundlessness.

Then Jake Lineker stood in his stirrups, to gain extra height, as he turned to peer back over the grim faced, unmoving group of men and women. And by the simple act of looking at the people caused them to remain silent. For certainly everyone obeyed his tacit edict, and no-one else swung out of the saddle as he did.

Even the overweight and overpainted Lydia Rice and the good looking young man with curly hair remained astride their horses until, down on the ground, Lineker gave them a curt nod. Then, as the fat woman and the man who was neither so young nor so good looking as he seemed at first glance dismounted, Lineker unhooked a coiled rope from his saddlehorn.

Not a cowpuncher's lariat with a conventional slipknot. Instead, a length of heavy-duty rope—the kind that could be found on any working farm or ranch—with one end fashioned into a running noose by a hangman's knot. No longer than ten feet when it was unfurled: which would be long enough to serve its intended purpose tonight.

'All right, Steele!' Jake Lineker yelled as he approached the front of the house. Halted six feet away from the door, between the sound window and the shattered one. Both showing chinks of dim lamplight through cracks in the drawn drapes. He waited for the Rice woman and her partner to flank him before he went on in the same commanding tone: 'We all know you're in there, you murderin' bastard! And you sure as hell know we're out here! So step on out into the open. Give an account of yourself! Same as these two strangers done!'

Steele was disconcerted: a state of mind he had consciously experienced before. But not so often he had learned how to handle the condition in the way that people more practised could. Despite the fact that he was completely out of sight of everybody, his first instinct was to mask his true feelings with something else. Which made him feel less vulnerable. In this case, it was easiest to choose anger. That his carefully laid plan had been ruined by the unexpected—half the damn town had come out here, instead of how he had wanted it to happen: just Lydia Rice and her partner.

But before his anger expanded into the loss of his temper beyond which he knew lay the impulse to reckless action, he was able to contract it into an ice-cold ball at the pit of his stomach. And to direct even this degree of rage inwards. For allowing himself to be so unsettled by the unexpected.

Which would never have happened in the old days. When he took each new situation, surprising or otherwise, in his stride.

The old days.

When all he had to lose was his life.

Which, if Trail's End was truly to be taken from him by those with legal title, was all he had to lose now.

'Show yourself, Steele!' Jake Lineker demanded.

'Yeah, do that, you crud!'

Lydia Rice's shrill voice was as menacing as the commanding tone of the bereaved man.

There was a chorus of growling agreement from the mounted group. From which only Tom Knight and Arlene Forrester abstained. Continued to sit, their heads bowed, in utter disconsolation.

'We all know you killed my girl, Steele!' Lineker challenged. 'The Widow Daltry caught you red handed, you murderin' bastard!'

There was another rumbling of voices, getting angrier. Silenced when a man Steele recognised as the rancher Gerry Chisholm, snarled:

'Come on, Steele! Step on out here and take what's comin' to you! Or we'll take care of your two helpers first!'

Everyone except for the trio aligned short of the front door turned to glower at Knight and the black woman. Until Lineker, running the coiled lynch rope faster through both his hands, began to demand:

'Come out, mister! Give yourself up or we surely will do that! Already give the nigger a hard time to find out you come here and so we won't——'

He broke off, clutched the rope tightly. As he and everyone else looked with the same intensity at the doorway of the house. Tom Knight and Arlene Forrester, too. For the sense of mass expectancy brought a degree of silence that penetrated into the private worlds of misery of the two prisoners. Compelled them to raise their bowed heads and look in the same direction.

In time to see the door swing slowly inward, so a lengthening and broadening shaft of low lamplight was laid across the yard.

The curly haired man shattered the silence when he yelled: 'Look out, he's got a gun!'

And hurled himself to the side, drew and fired his Colt. With such smooth speed Steele was certain this had to be the professional gunslinger Tom Knight had seen in San Francisco.

'My God, that ain't Steele! That's the dimwit you——' Lydia Rice broke off.

'It's Baxter!' Huey Attrill cut in, tone shrill with horror. 'You killed the——'

'Right!' Steele snarled. Refused to be disconcerted by the mysterious opening of the house door. As the barn doors he had thrown open crashed back against the wall to either side. And he stepped out over the threshold into the bright moonlight. Added: 'I needed somebody to give me the ghost of a chance.'

14

The sudden uproar of raised voices panicked some of the horses, already spooked by the gunshot. Which Curly had exploded after his spring to the side sent the cursing Jake Lineker sprawling to the ground.

So just a few of the mounted men and women had the opportunity to catch more than a fleeting glimpse of what happened next: the rest having to concentrate on bringing their rearing, shying horses back under control.

But Lineker, risen up on to one knee, saw it. And so did Lydia Rice, her feet rooted to the spot by the scene within the house: but with enough presence of mind to wrench her head around. Stare toward the barn doorway.

Curly remained in the gunfighter's crouch for a fraction of a second after hearing Steele's voice. But recovered from the shock of the scene beyond the house doorway at the same instant as the woman. Swung his entire body around, gun hand arcing fastest. Thumbed back the hammer as part of the same fluid move.

The icy ball at the pit of Steele's stomach expanded to control his entire being. Killed any impulse to heated recklessness. Kept his actions composed without hampering their smooth speed. So he had the Colt Hartford down from his shoulder, levelled from the hip, hammer back, while Curly was a part of a second short of finding his target with the handgun.

The second gunshot exploded. This time the bullet tunnelled through living flesh: drilled into Curly's heart. And the force of its impact sent him staggering backwards with a grunt, arms hurled sideways, Colt falling from his convulsing hand.

Jake Lineker rose and whirled, scuttled out of the path of the dead man on his feet. Only just avoided being beneath the corpse when it crashed heavily to the ground.

'He's done it again!' Lydia Rice shrieked.

And despite the icy calm that had gripped Steele since he regained control of his emotions, he felt a sense of *dêjà vu*. Fleetingly recalled the scene out back of the church when the Widow Daltry had screamed much the same thing. But now the Rice woman went on in a far different vein:

'Get him! Get the bastard! You saw him! He just shot my brother! Kill him! Shoot down that friggin' murderer!'

The people of Providence seldom carried guns. Unless officially deputised by Len Fallows into a posse. Or, it was now apparent, were stirred up into forming a lynch mob.

Michael Morrison, Gerry Chisholm and two men who Steele knew worked farms to the east of town, drew revolvers or reached to clutch the frames of booted rifles. But the Virginian took the chance he understood these kind of people well enough: to risk sloping the Colt Hartford to his shoulder again. Reckoned these men and their fellow citizens would have sufficient self control not to fire their guns unless they were threatened. With the rifle at his shoulder, they were not.

Lydia Rice suddenly broke off. And wrenched her head away from the impassive Virginian to glare at the mounted townspeople. Where the men with drawn revolvers no longer aimed them, those who had reached for rifles let them remain in the boots. Then she demanded to know, less stridently:

'What's the matter with you friggin' people? We came out here to see he paid for all the murderin' he's done. Now he's killed Jack. And you sit there like Goddamn corpses yourself. What the frig are you waitin' for?'

She looked away from them. To Steele, Jake Lineker, her dead brother, then into the house. Pointed a shaking hand and yelled bitterly: 'Look! Steele even cut the throat of that lamebrain he was supposed to think so much of! Just to pull some kinda lousy trick that made——'

Lineker had moved alongside her so he could look into the house. And several people leaned down in their saddles, to see better over the threshold. This as the bearded farmer asked evenly:

'Billy's throat's cut, lady? How the hell do you know that?'

Steele vented a soft sigh as the muscle-aching tension drained out of him.

'Sonofabitch!' Huey Attrill growled.

'Oh, my God!' Ellie Lineker gasped.

Tom Knight excitedly tried to call the attention of Arlene Forrester to what held the others. But the black woman merely cast a tear-blurred glance through the doorway. Too grief-stricken by the death of Billy Baxter to feel any sense of relief the manner of his dying was maybe going to keep Steele's head out of a lynch noose: get herself and Knight out of further trouble.

'Lady?' Lineker insisted, the harshness of his tone silencing the mounting volume of questioning voices.

And the single word caused a jolt to shudder through the fleshy frame of Lydia Rice. Like the demand had palpable substance that crashed into her. As hard as the bullet which moments ago killed her brother.

But she continued to stare fixedly into the room. Which had been cleaned of all traces of the mess which she and Jack had left. Cleaned for two reasons. Primarily the chore had served to calm Steele's nerves and help him retain control of his bitter anger while he waited. But, also, he had felt strongly that if he were to lose his life after losing everything that made living worthwhile, he had no wish to die in the squalor which other people had brought to his home.

Then, after he finished the cleaning up, he arranged for Billy Baxter to have a hand in the killing of those who had killed him. As part of a simple plan, maybe designed by a slightly unbalanced mind. Which had seemed about to go badly wrong when the lynch mob showed up.

'It's what I want to know, too,' Len Fallows said grimly. This as he stepped out into the yard, right hand draped over the butt of his holstered revolver.

The sheriff's sudden appearance caused another shock wave to go through the perplexed and nervous crowd. And horses scraped at the ground as they sensed human unease and reacted with the equine variety.

While Steele sighed softly again, as the mystery of the opening door was solved.

Fallows went on: 'Like you can see, ma'am. Steele dressed up Billy in a set of his own clothes, including a kerchief. Not possible to spot how the poor guy was killed. Hours before your brother pumped a bullet into the corpse.'

There was a pause of perhaps two stretched seconds. Then:

'It was Jack!' Lydia Rice blurted. Whirled to point a rock-steady accusing finger at the spreadeagled dead man. 'The lamebrain, he came out here to feed the stock, he said. And milk the cow. We told him we'd take care of all that, and we thought he'd took off. But he went nosin' around in the barn. Saw we'd butchered the animals. Started to holler. Jack brought him in the house when he wouldn't quiet down. And . . . Shit, Jack had one hell of a bad temper!'

Fallows started to raise his hand from his holstered revolver toward his head, recalling his own painful experience of the dead man's violent streak.

A loud sob escaped Arlene Forrester's throat, but then she regained enough self-control to weep silently.

'What about my girl?' Jake Lineker said in low but dangerous tones. Shot a glance at his wife. 'Our daughter? What happened?'

He began to run the coil of rope through his hands again. Licking his thick lips above his beard. Wetting them as tears wet his wife's sunken cheeks.

Lydia Rice blurted: 'That was Jack's idea, mister! I didn't have nothin' . . . If he hadn't shown up when he did, Elmer and me . . . We wouldn't have——'

'Our daughter!' Lineker repeated with menace, the rope coil circling faster by the moment.

The business-suited Archer and Decker, both shamefaced, began hurriedly to untie the ropes which bound the wrists of Arlene and Knight to their saddlehorns. Knight was softly snarling something to the pair of storekeepers. While the black woman stared into the middle distance with glistening eyes.

'Start with your husband,' Fallows countermanded coldly. Directed a warning glare at Lineker when the bearded farmer vented a growl of anger. Reminded pointedly: 'Seems to me, Jake, you and the rest of this sorry bunch of vigilantes came close to lynching an innocent man: on account of not getting all the facts.'

The agreement now voiced by most of the mounted townspeople was low-keyed, remorseful. And Lineker abruptly flung the rope to the ground, whirled to go stand beside his wife. Who still wept as silently as Arlene, both women hunched in their saddles.

'Elmer wasn't my husband,' Lydia Rice revealed. Stared down at the dusty ground immediately in front of her. 'But I took his name. Him and me... We were just a couple of down on our luck theatricals. Happened to hear about what this guy named Steele had done. Moved in on a place that didn't belong to him and fixed it up so——'

She lifted her head, to look across at the barn doorway. Was just mildly surprised, like everyone else, not to see the Virginian standing there. Then she shrugged her bulky shoulders. Recaptured mass attention as she went on:

'Heard what he'd done at this place that didn't belong to him. Heard how it used to be owned by somebody called Sanderson. That really is my true name: Lydia Sanderson. But I ain't no relation, I know that for sure. But Elmer and me figured we'd try to swing it so we'd claim title to the place. Now it was all done up. Sell it and make a pile. Would've, too, maybe. If I hadn't written a letter to my kid brother. To ask him to throw in with us. In the event we needed the kind of help he could give... In handlin' people.'

'Your brother?' Tom Knight interrupted, rubbing his

wrists where the tight ropes had pained him. 'Did he get called Curly up in San Francisco? A couple of years or so back?'

The query intrigued some people: aroused irritable impatience in others. Lydia Rice answered sourly after a glance down at the dead man:

'He was known as Curly everywhere he hired his fast gun, mister. As his sister, I guess I was the only person ever called him Jack these days.'

'So he came to town, and I told him how to get out here to Trail's End?' Fallows prompted, one of the impatient listeners.

'Yeah. Jack showed up. And Elmer and me, we got to fightin' about cuttin' my brother in. Elmer and me, we always fought. About every damn thing. Jack went to look over the spread, and Elmer and me, we carried on fightin'. It was a bad one. And my share of the family temper came out strong. I grabbed Elmer's gun and took a shot at him. Missed him the first time. Not the second.'

She looked pensively toward the shattered window, maybe saw for the first time that Steele had got rid of the shards of glass during his cleaning chores.

'What Adam Steele said about getting jumped by somebody?' Fallows asked. 'It was the truth?'

She nodded. 'Jack spotted him headin' on to the place. Was right there, and he jumped him just as I killed Elmer. Right in time to stick him with the killin'.'

'Why our daughter?' Ellie Lineker pressed, her voice thick, as she reached down a hand to clutch a broad shoulder of her husband.

After she had looked quizzically at Fallows, who remained silent, Lydia Rice said in reply: 'Jack was still out here. Hid in the barn when I went to town. To bring out the sheriff. And some others that came with him. Jack saw how things were shapin' to get Steele free. But, of course, he couldn't do nothin' to stop it. Since he was supposed to have moved on.

'But he trailed Steele to town, saw him let into the roomin' house. Then he came back here and we talked. Figured it was best to let things be for a while. Steele on the run, that made him look real guilty. But we figured we should keep an eye on him. So Jack went back into town this mornin'. Got there just as the woman sneaked Steele out of the roomin' house. While the sheriff was raisin' a ruckus. Followed them to the church.'

'You still ain't told us why our girl was killed that way,' Jake Lineker insisted. Raised his hand to put it upon that of his wife's where it rested on his shoulder. 'There wasn't no need, seems to me, to . . .'

'Jack was comin' back out here,' Lydia Rice answered when the big farmer's voice faltered. 'When he heard how it was the wo—your daughter—snitched to the sheriff in a note where Steele was hid. Jack didn't know what was behind that, but he figured if she turned up murdered . . . Murdered in a bad way, then everyone was bound to think Steele——'

'Quite so, lady, we can see that,' Huey Attrill said. Looked up from the sheaf of paper on which he had been hurriedly scribbling details of the confession.

It signalled a burst of shocked exclamations from the townspeople. Many of them figuring the words *disgusting, brutal, awful, violent* and *tragic*. Then, in the wake of shock, came anger. And many of the riders moved to swing out of their saddles. Until, as he stepped in front of the cowering Lydia Rice and draped a hand over his revolver, the glowering Fallows snarled:

'It's pretty damn disgusting the way you took Arlene Forrester and Tom Knight out of my cells! And locked me up! A matter of degree, that's all! I oughta arrest the whole damn bunch that came out here to take the law into your own hands!'

'I just came along to get a report for the——' Attrill began to defend.

Harold Archer excused: 'After what happened to Susannah, we were driven a little crazy, Len.'

'That's what I'm making allowances for,' the lawman retorted grimly, both the expression on his rough-hewn face and the tone of his voice revealing the strain he was under to keep his rage in check. 'You people better thank your lucky stars Lavinia Attwood placed common sense and civic duty before emotion. And let me out. So I could come here after you. Keep you from going through with what you had in mind!'

The Virginian had gone to the rear of the house when he left the barn doorway. Stood on the bank of the low water Timber Creek to listen to the woman confess her involvement in three killings. Two of which, in the old days, would have compelled him to kill her at the first opportunity. Or maybe all three: since the blasting of Elmer Rice had first caused him to be hunted by his fellow citizens.

But, once more, he had to remind himself the old days were gone: there was no reason to return to the way he had been then. Now he had not lost Trail's End.

He went into the house then, through the back door. The same way Len Fallows must have entered, after approaching the place silently, on foot. For there was no horse to be seen.

From within the dimly lamplit room, the Virginian heard many of the riders in the yard turn their mounts and head slowly away over the track between the crop fields. This as he went to the table which he had dragged in line with the front door. Where Billy still sat, propped in a chair, despite taking Jack Sanderson's bullet in his unfeeling chest. His right hand fisted around the old Colt which was usually kept in the barn. The revolver barrel resting on a book so the muzzle was aimed at the open doorway.

Where Len Fallows now showed himself on the threshold again: as hard faced as at any time since he stepped out over it minutes ago.

'He sure as hell fooled me, Steele,' the lawman said with a slight shake of his head. 'When I first sneaked in and saw him sitting there like that. If I was of a mind, I'd have shot him and been certain I was shooting you.'

'It didn't work out like I planned, but it worked out,' Steele answered. Took the old revolver out of the dead fingers.

'Glad I was able to have a hand in stopping what would have been a grave miscarriage of justice, Steele.'

Len Fallows was embarrassed. Perhaps because of how a section of the townspeople had acted. Or because he felt uncomfortable at needing to side with the Virginian. More likely, because he realised the comment sounded so pompous.

'Grateful to you.'

'You need a hand with anything here?'

'Reckon to bury Billy on Trail's End, sheriff. It was the place he enjoyed being when he was a kid. And lately. Handle that myself. They buried Rice out at the side of the house. Like to have him taken care of by the Broadwater undertakers?'

Fallows nodded. 'Be taking the woman up there tomorrow. The court's sitting this week. I'll have——'

'Grateful to you.'

Lydia Rice, her voice tremulous with a brand of emotion that had not been heard while she was confessing, asked from out in the yard: 'What about my brother's remains?'

'The Broadwater undertakers can take him, too,' Steele replied to the lawman's questioning look. 'Meantime, I'll put his carcase in the barn with the rest of the dead animals.'

Fallows nodded and stepped out of the house. Said: 'Okay, Tom. Thanks, I'll take charge of her now. My horse's just a short way down the spur.'

Tom Knight appeared in the doorway, both hands behind his back. Announced: 'Arlene's gone to do some private weepin' over Billy at her own place. She told me to tell you.'

'What? Oh, yeah. Fine.'

Knight brought his hands into view, to show he was clutching a bottle of whiskey in each. 'If you was a drinkin' man, Steele . . . Me and you, we could make use of this liquor the woman and her gunslinger brother went to Harry Krim's place to get tonight. But since you don't touch the stuff . . ? I found it in his saddlebags.'

'Right, I don't touch it any more. You're welcome to it. Do something for me?'

Knight was as renowned in Providence for his laziness as for his liking for liquor. With a glance at the corpse, he responded without enthusiasm: 'Sure.'

'Since you're leaving, be grateful if you'll . . .

. . . CLOSE THE DOOR.'*

* *As it is closed on this story. But Adam Steele will re-emerge in the next book of the series.*

GEORGE G. GILMAN

ADAM STEELE
NO. 40 THE SUNSET RIDE

This time he'd really been left holding the baby.

Somewhere between the Mojave Desert and the Sierra Nevadas, a trailside encounter with sudden death was about to force Adam Steele into learning a whole new set of survival skills.

Like diaper-changing and hustling up a mess of warm milk. Like soothing and lulling and watching the cradle.

Just the sort of thing to take a man's mind off the night-time dangers of outlaw territory.

And get him killed.

NEW ENGLISH LIBRARY

GEORGE G. GILMAN

ADAM STEELE
NO 41: THE KILLING STRAIN

Trail's End, it was called. Not the sort of place to end up: land abandoned, ownership obscure, farmstead falling down, no crops, no stock.

But to Adam Steele it looked like it might be the road to the future. Spread out along the Californian foothills of the High Sierras, he could see it as a thriving horse ranch, and him thriving with it.

But when he woke up to uninvited house guests standing over him, one covering him with a rifle and the other, the one with the baseball bat, aiming to turn Steele's head into a Virginia hamburger, it was the present that was mostly on his mind.

NEW ENGLISH LIBRARY